FOOL'S GOLD

Also by Zilpha Keatley Snyder

FOOL'S GOLD

Zilpha Keatley Snyder

Delacorte
Press

Published by
Delacorte Press
Bantam Doubleday Dell Publishing Group, Inc.
666 Fifth Avenue
New York, New York 10103

Library of Congress Cataloging in Publication Data

Snyder, Zilpha Keatley.
    Fool's gold / Zilpha Keatley Snyder.
        p.   cm.
    Summary: Reluctant to admit that he suffers
from claustrophobia and anxious not to alienate
his friends, Rudy tries to find a way to distract
them from pursuing their plan of exploring an
abandoned gold mine.
    ISBN 0-385-30908-2
    [1. Friendship—Fiction.   2. Phobias—Fiction.
3. Gold mines and mining—Fiction.   4. Single-
parent family—Fiction.]   I. Title.
PZ7.S68522Fo   1993
[Fic]—dc20   92-24892
                                              CIP
                                               AC

Manufactured in the United States of America
April 1993

10 9 8 7 6 5 4 3 2 1
BVG

To George Nicholson,
with admiration and appreciation

Chapter 1

THE ONLY LIGHT came from a small flickering flame. There was no sound except for the faint gurgle of something slimy that oozed down the walls and trickled underfoot. He was all alone. The others had been with him only a moment before, but now they had disappeared. He turned back, shouting their names, but there was no answer. He shouted again and the sound returned to him in a jabbering chorus. Something, perhaps his own gasping breath, disturbed the tiny flame and it sank lower, wavered, and as he tried desperately to shield it with his cupped hands, died completely away. The heavy, smothering darkness was suddenly shaken by a terrible sound. Someone was screaming.

"Rudy. What is it? Was that you?"

1

For a moment his mother's voice blended with the blind panic of the dream, but then his eyes opened and relief surged through him. It was only a nightmare—and not a new one. Only a slightly different version of a dream he'd been having over and over again since early spring. Some of them hadn't been too bad, but this one had been a real killer. Sitting up, he struggled to focus his sleep-blurred eyes and to force his lips into something like a smile.

"Wow!" he said. "Did I yell? Yeah, I guess I did."

His mother was standing in the door in her nightgown, her eyes wide and startled in her sleep-rumpled face. "What is it, Rudy? Did you have another nightmare?"

"Yeah." He took a deep breath, shook his head to clear it, and managed a slightly more typical grin. "Yeah. A real killer this time. X-rated." His grin widened. "Or at least 'parental discretion advised.' " Doing a pathetic little-kid face, he whined, "How come you let me watch that kind of stuff, Mom?"

Sitting down on the edge of his bed, Natasha put her hand on his arm. "What were you dreaming about?"

Rudy rolled his eyes thoughtfully and then shook his head and shrugged, hoping to give the impression that he couldn't remember, without actually having to lie about it. He didn't want to get into what the dreams were like, because that would be certain to bring up—

"Why do you suppose you've been having so many nightmares lately?"

There it was—the one question he didn't dare get into. Not with anyone—and particularly not with his mother. Trying desperately to think of a good way to avoid answering, he stared at his mother's face. Usually Natasha was pretty good-looking for her age, which was around thirty-three, but at the moment her face was puffy with sleep and bare of makeup and her hair looked as if it had been combed with an eggbeater.

"Arrghh!" he said, cringing back against the headboard. "The invasion of the living dead."

Her reaction was typical—a glare that gradually turned into a giggle. If you could get Natasha to laugh she usually forgot about doing the stern-parent bit. She swatted at him, got up off his bed, and went out. At the door she stopped and said, "Well, I might as well stay up. It's past seven and I promised Frank I'd be at the store at eight thirty for the back-room inventory. Let the girls sleep a little longer. And don't forget to remind them about this afternoon. Okay?"

Rudy said okay and then collapsed under the blankets—to give himself time to shake off the last dark shadows of the dream. It took a few minutes and some careful thought control. The thought control went like this: *Don't even think about the nightmares —or what's causing them. Think about something really great instead—something like my impersonation of Michael Jackson at the Graduates Talent Assembly last Thursday—and how everyone had cracked up— even solemn old Stephanie.* Yeah, that helped. Thinking about old deadpan Stephanie's giggle wiped out all kinds of gruesome memories—even memories of . . . *Don't think about it.*

It took a while, but it worked. By the time he climbed out of bed he was himself again even though the whole thing—the nightmares and what he knew was causing them—was sneaking in and out of his conscious mind as he began his Saturday morning breakfast routine. Like a robot operating on only one cylinder he got out the cereal and milk, cleaned up the mess where Ophelia (the poodle) had barfed on the floor, and even came up with a new threat to make his sisters stop fighting.

"Death!" he yelled suddenly when the usual screams and thuds and high-pitched yelps finally began to get through to him. The yelps were from Ophelia, who always got hysterical when Moira and Margot started fighting—like about a dozen times a day. "Death! Terminal death, if you two don't chill out and eat your breakfast."

To his surprise it worked. His sisters, half sisters, that is, dropped their weapons—a dust mop and a fly-swatter—and sat down at the table. Moira, the skinny brown-haired one, was eight and the oldest by one year, but they were a fairly even match. Margot, blonder and chunkier, was fiercer and could punch harder, but Moira was quicker on her feet and a lot sneakier.

"Terminal death?" Moira whispered.

Margot nodded. "Terminal."

They both looked at Rudy with Barbie-doll eyes while he stared back, giving them his Nazi-officer bit, chin jutted out and eyes narrowed to cruel slits.

For a moment a stranger might have thought that he'd really scared them, but he knew better. They were too used to him. They'd had too much experience with the Rudolph Drummond Baby-sitting Method, which

4

had always depended on all kinds of dramatic impersonations and lots of creative threats.

Moira's round blue eyes finally blinked. "What
does terminal mean?" she asked.

"Shhh!" he whispered, then, doing his German
accent, "Don't zay anyzing. Zee enemy iss listening."

That gave them something to think about. They
were still glancing nervously over their shoulders
when Rudy tuned them out again and went back to
cleaning up the breakfast mess, and to his own
thoughts and problems. The problems were definitely
taking over and he was feeling more and more misera-
ble as he scrubbed out the sink and swept up the cereal
that had been spilled during the fight. It wasn't until
he had finished and was putting away the broom that
he began to cheer up.

The mirror helped. Natasha had mounted a mirror
on the broom cupboard door and it was when he
caught sight of his reflection that he finally began to
snap out of it. He had to admit that one thing he did
have going for him was his looks. Of course, he wasn't
exactly muscle-bound, but his face was not all that
bad, that was for sure—a little bit narrow and bony
maybe, but with great eyebrows and eyes and . . . He
was turning his head to study his best camera angle
when somebody giggled.

Rudy turned to see the M and M's (Rudy often
referred to Margot and Moira as the M and M's) watching from the hall doorway. He slammed the closet door
and went after them doing a Frankenstein number—
hunched shoulders and dragging foot—but as soon as
they disappeared down the hall, shrieking and gig-

gling, he dropped the chase and headed for the front porch to see if anything had changed overnight.

Nothing had. The street was still narrow and twisting. Next door, at the big old Woodbury house, the tin roof was still rusting away, and nothing grand and exciting had sprung up overnight on any of the vacant lots. Well, maybe tomorrow. Or the day after that. Or five years from now. Or fifty.

He sniffed the air. Nothing new and different there either. Just a typical June morning in the awesomely quaint and historic California gold-rush town of Pyramid Hill in the beautiful Sierra foothills. At the present time, 8:32 A.M. plus 17 seconds, according to his state-of-the-art Timex watch—his graduation present— the air was still fresh and fairly cool. However, a bright sun was clearing the mountain ridges to the east, and from almost fourteen long years of experience he knew that hot and dusty were just around the corner.

He had just started to go back in the front door when, warned by the sound of screaming voices and running feet, he jumped back barely in time to avoid becoming a traffic victim. A hit-and-run by two girls and a poodle.

Still plastered back against the veranda wall, he yelled, "Margot! Moira! Come back here. I forgot to tell you something."

They heard him all right, but they went on running, down the porch steps and out onto the street, with Ophelia right behind them barking her crazy head off.

Actors need to be able to project their voices, and great projection was another of Rudy's natural acting talents. Taking a deep breath and squinching his eyes shut with the effort, he let loose a mega-force bellow. *"Stop!"*

When he opened his eyes the M and M's were frozen in mid-step, with Moira still holding up one fist and Margot still clinging to the back of Moira's T-shirt. The screaming had stopped and so had the yapping. Rudy strode across the porch. On the top step he folded his arms and stared down sternly at his sisters.

"All right, you hoodlums," he said, a judge looking down from the bench at guilty prisoners. "The verdict is in. Six months for disturbing the peace! And if you tear that shirt, Margot, you're going to get five years at hard labor."

Margot only tightened her hold. "But she took all the money, and half of it's mine. Mom said so."

Moira's smile was full of phony sisterly understanding. "I know it's half yours. I was just going to keep it till lunchtime. So you wouldn't lose it."

Rudy was beginning to pry Margot off the T-shirt when, from next door, there was the sudden sound of a screen door slamming and scuffling footsteps.

"Rudy. Rudy Drummond. What's going on, boy? Somebody committing mayhem on your premises?"

Murphy Woodbury was leaning over the railing in his usual ratty old jeans and undershirt, his gray hair standing up in quivering corkscrews. Under his sagging eyelids his eyes were, as always, shiny with curiosity. "What was all that screaming and yelling I just heard?" he asked.

Rudy sighed and, grabbing each of his sisters by a

wrist, he turned back, pulling them after him, with Margot still attached to the back of Moira's shirt.

Murph, who was probably around sixty years old, had lived most of his life in the big old rambling house next door to Rudy. The Woodburys went back to the original gold-rush pioneers and Murph's father and grandfather had lived there before him. According to Natasha, Murph had gone away to live in a city for a while when he was a young man and he'd had a wife with him when he came back. But the wife hated living in Pyramid and there had been a divorce, and Murph went on living alone in the old Woodbury house. Murph made his living by renting some property he owned in town—which was a good thing, since he never seemed to make any money at either of his other two jobs. Murph's jobs, to hear him tell it, were "author" and "student of humanity." Which meant that he spent a few minutes now and then banging away on his ancient typewriter, and the rest of his time doing what *he* called studying humanity. There were other people in town, a lot of them in fact, who called it snooping into other people's business. But Rudy had never minded Murph's curiosity—not until lately, anyway.

He and Murph had always spent lots of time together. For one thing Murph was always around, since he didn't go to work every day like most people, and for another he knew a lot about nearly everything, and there wasn't anything he didn't know about Pyramid Hill and everyone who lived there. And he was a great storyteller. Rudy couldn't even begin to count the hours he'd spent in Murph's backyard or kitchen with

Murph helping on one of Rudy's research projects. Or else eating—Murph was a great cook—or just talking. In those days visiting Murph had been one of Rudy's favorite pastimes. But sometimes, particularly recently, his snooping got on Rudy's nerves.

"Nothing important," Rudy said. "Just these two nerds fighting again."

Murph chuckled. "No. That can't be true. Two such lovely little ladies actually engaging in physical combat? You must have been mistaken."

Murph was full of it. No one who lived within a block of the M and M's could help but know how much they "engaged in physical combat." But the "lovely ladies" bit did seem to work on Margot at least, who smiled sheepishly, let go of Moira's T-shirt, and put her hands behind her back.

Not to be outdone, Moira began giving Murph her movie-star special smile. "You're right, Mr. Woodbury. We weren't fighting. At least I wasn't. I was just trying to keep Margot from losing her lunch money." She edged closer to the porch railing and whispered behind her hand. "She loses tons of money all the time."

"Is that right?" Murph whispered back. "Tell me about it. How much money would you say your sister has lost this last month?"

Moira shrugged. "Lots. A thousand dollars, maybe."

"I see." Murph nodded solemnly. "That's a lot all right. Fancy a little girl like her losing that much money." He winked at Rudy, which was probably supposed to mean that Moira's wild stories were harmless and amusing, but Murph didn't have to live with them every day. Rudy didn't wink back. Lately the M and M's had been getting on his nerves even more than Murph was.

"Here," Rudy said, prying the money out of Moira's fist and giving half of it to Margot. "Now, don't lose it. And you guys are supposed to come back here right after lunch. You're only going to stay at Eleanora's in the mornings from now on. That's what I was supposed to tell you. Mom said she told you, but you'd probably forget if I didn't remind you."

"I remembered," Moira said.

"I did too," Margot said. "I remembered it better than she did. I even remembered that Mom said you were going to baby-sit us every afternoon, and read to us and play games too."

"Right." Rudy couldn't keep a certain amount of bitterness out of his voice. "Every afternoon I'm good old big-brother Rudy, the baby-sitter. But every morning at"—he glanced at his watch—"nine o'clock I turn into a bloodsucking vampire. So get out—before I start getting hungry." He jumped at them, doing a fangs and claws bit, but they ignored him and started off down the street still glaring at each other. It wouldn't be long, however, before they'd forget it and be best friends again—until the next declaration of war.

"Natasha working today?" Murph asked.

"Sure. And tomorrow too. Like always." Natasha worked in Fraser's Antique Store, which, because of the tourist trade in Pyramid Hill, was always open on weekends. It was a lousy job for a mother. In fact, it was a lousy job in a lot of ways and she hated it, but as she was always saying, with three kids to raise all by herself, what was she going to do?

"Well, it's a lousy job," Murph said, like an echo of Rudy's thoughts. He sighed and shook his head. Murph had always been like a father to Natasha, going out of his way to help her whenever he could. Especially when she'd really needed help, like when she came back to Pyramid Hill pregnant with Rudy, and later when she was married to Art Mumford. Not to mention right after he went off and left her alone with three kids to take care of.

Murph sighed again and then suddenly switched to his usual straggly old grin. "Well now," he said. "Speaking of getting hungry, I haven't had breakfast yet. How about joining me in an old-fashioned chuck wagon breakfast?" Of course, Rudy had just eaten, but only cold cereal, and Murph was practically famous for his huge cowboy breakfasts just loaded with delicious calories and cholesterol.

Tipping up an imaginary Stetson and squinting his eyes, Rudy became Windy Dayes, one of his most famous impersonations. Windy was a favorite local character, a weather-beaten old cowboy who spent his time hanging around downtown, bending people's ears with long-winded cowboy-type stories. Lots of people tried to imitate Windy, but no one could do it as well as Rudy. So now he hitched up his pants, drawled, "Waal now, pardner, ah don't mahnd if I dew," and bowlegged it toward Murph's back door.

11

Chapter 2

IN THE CLUTTERED OLD KITCHEN Rudy sat down at the round oak table while Murph puttered around, putting strips of bacon in the frying pan and cracking some eggs. He was pouring pancake batter on the grill when he started in on the baby-sitting thing.

"So you're going to be spending a lot of time baby-sitting your sisters this summer? Natasha told me about it. Said you volunteered."

Rudy shrugged. "Just in the afternoons. Wednesday through Sunday."

"That's going to help Natasha a lot. Save her quite a bit of money too. Right noble offer on your part."

Rudy shrugged again and said nothing. He wasn't going to be drawn into explaining why he'd volunteered his services. It was one question that nosy old Murphy Woodbury would just have to guess about.

After a few moments of silence Murph went on about the M and M's. "So, this time the battling ballerinas were fighting about money," he said. "It's always something, isn't it?"

"Some ballerinas," Rudy said. As far as he could see neither of his sisters had much natural talent, but they'd been taking ballet almost since they started walking and they were always tearing around the yard in ratty tutus and doing clutzy jetés and arabesques up and down the veranda. But Natasha seemed to think they were really talented.

The thing was that Natasha—whose real first name had been Linda before she changed it—had been a ballet dancer before she started having kids and had to give it up. But she kept her hand in by practicing almost every day, not to mention naming her kids after famous dancers. She also taught some, but since there wasn't too much interest in ballet in Pyramid Hill, she mostly just taught her own kids. Including Rudy at one time, until he found out how some people in Pyramid felt about boys taking ballet.

"I don't see why Natasha doesn't just forget about the whole ballet thing," Rudy said. "It's just a waste of everybody's time."

"Well now, I wouldn't say that. Not at all. I think your mother has been very brave to hang on to her dream that way even though she's had such a hard time and—"

Rudy laughed. "Okay, okay, I take it back." He knew better than to criticize Natasha even a little when

Murph was around. "But I still think trying to make ballerinas out of the M and M's is a waste of time."

Murph chuckled. "Oh, well. It gives them something to do, doesn't it?"

"Not to mention something else to fight about," Rudy said, with more bitterness than usual. "It's the truth. Every time they practice it turns into a big blowup. You know—about who's wearing whose leotards, or hogging too much room at the barre, or who just pirouetted into somebody else's space."

Murph chuckled again, but after he put the plates on the table and sat down, he looked at Rudy and stopped smiling.

"Hmm," he said. "A bit downcast and melancholy at the moment, aren't we, Rudy Drummond? Particularly when one considers that this very morning marks the arrival of summer vacation and three months of relative freedom."

"Yeah," he said. "Summer vacation. Great! I'm all excited."

Murph poured some cream in his coffee, stirred it, and then sipped without taking his eyes off Rudy. Finally he asked, "Could all this uncharacteristic lack of good cheer have something to do with Barnaby Crookshank?"

For a crazy moment Rudy thought Murph actually knew. His mind racing, he took a big bite of pancake and pretended to be too busy chewing to say anything. It was true that Murph sometimes seemed to be able to tune in on things that most people would miss, but that didn't mean he could really read minds. And if you ruled out actual mind reading—just how much could he possibly know?

"Ahem." Murph cleared his throat and Rudy swallowed hard and came back to the question.

"No," Rudy said. "No. Why should the fact that I'm not exactly flipping over school's being out have anything to do with Barney? It's just that . . . It's just that . . . Well, it's too hot in Pyramid in the summertime. And too many tourists. And there's practically nothing for guys my age to do in this one-horse town in the summertime. I don't know. Maybe I'm just bored."

Murph's smile said that he knew Rudy was talking nonsense. And it was true, of course. Nobody knew better than Murph just how good Rudy had always been at thinking up things to do, or to build, or to do research on. Murph had been particularly involved in the research projects—like tracing the roots of some of the Pyramid Hill families who went back to the gold rush, or the biography of Will Rogers, or the one on snake charmers in India. And, of course, the research on the lives of other talented or famous people who had been illegitimate. Murph had been especially helpful with the Famous Bastards project.

So it *was* nonsense to pretend the problem was simple boredom, and Rudy was about to admit it by shrugging sheepishly when Murph's smile suddenly turned into a quizzical expression that said, "So come on, tell me what's really bothering you." And that was none of his business.

"Look, Murph," Rudy said. "Stop bugging me. Nothing's wrong. All right?"

"Sure thing," Murph said. He got up and puttered around the stove for a while, chatting about the pancakes and whether they were up to his usual standard, as if he'd forgotten all about giving Rudy the third degree. But as soon as he sat down again he said, right out of the blue, "So, who is this Lewis kid? Ty, I think they call him. The one with the spiky hair." Sometimes it really did seem like Murph Woodbury was a mind reader.

"Tyler Lewis?" Rudy said. "What's he got to do with it?"

"I don't know. I'm asking you. I've just seen him around a lot lately. Sometimes with you and Barney and sometimes just with Barney."

"Yeah," Rudy said. "Well, he's just this dude from Southern California. L.A., I think. His folks moved up here last summer to start a new real estate business. He's in some classes with Barney and me. He's . . . What can I tell you about Ty Lewis?" Rudy's laugh felt a little bit forced. "Well, to put it in Ty-wanese . . . he's a rude dude."

"Ty-wanese?" Murph asked.

"That's what Barney and I call the way Ty talks. Ty uses a lot of slang. I mean, when Ty first started hanging out with Barney and me, half the time we couldn't figure out what he was talking about. So we started saying he spoke 'Ty-wanese.' Get it?"

Murph nodded. "Got it. So this new kid speaks a language all his own. And he's rude?"

Rudy laughed. "Rude means great. In Ty-wanese, that is. Great. Awesome. Like, you say 'Hey, that is one really rude jacket'—or whatever. And 'dude.' Well, everyone is 'dude' to Ty. Even girls."

"I see," Murph said in the supersolemn way that looked like he was taking something extraseriously but really meant just the opposite.

They ate in silence for a few minutes before Rudy asked again, "Why'd you bring Ty up? What's he got to do with anything?"

Murph shrugged. "I don't know. Maybe I'm way off base, but it's just that you and Barney have been close for so long, and now this new kid comes along. Thought maybe the two of them have been ganging up on you, or something."

Rudy made a surprised face and asked, "What makes you think that?"

"Well, partly something I overheard the other day, I guess," Murph said. "When the three of you were sitting on your veranda. Sounded to me like this Ty kid was trying to put you down, and maybe Barney was going along with it, at least a little."

"Aha!" Rudy said, shaking his finger at Murph. "You've been 'studying humanity' again. Where were you this time? At a keyhole? Or peeking through the curtains?"

Murph grinned. "Don't recall. But there *was* some teasing going on, wasn't there?"

"Nothing important, I guess. I can't remember." Rudy tried to look unconcerned even though a small dark cloud of worry had suddenly floated into the back of his mind. "Er—what was it exactly that you heard?"

"I don't recall the exact words but"—Murph paused while he poked at the last of the hash brown potatoes on his plate—"the Lewis kid seemed to be carrying on about you objecting to something they were planning to do."

The small dark cloud suddenly mushroomed. "Planning?" Rudy asked.

"Um." Murph nodded. "Some sort of a money-making project, I gathered. Didn't hear what exactly." The cloud dwindled. "The Ty kid started jumping around flapping his elbows. Made it harder to make out what he was saying."

"Yeah." Rudy shrugged. "That was supposed to be me."

Murph looked puzzled. "The flapping elbows meant you? Why's that?"

Sometimes Murph was unbelievably out of it. "A chicken." Rudy explained with exaggerated patience. "When you do this"—Rudy flapped his elbows— "that's supposed to mean chicken, Murph. That's me, according to Ty. He gets on my case a little sometimes. But I get on his too. It's no big deal."

"Well, why was he calling you chicken? If I'm not being too curious."

Rudy shrugged. "Yeah, you're being too curious. But then, what else is new? Murphy P. Woodbury is famous for being too curious. Right?"

"Guilty as charged," Murph said, grinning. "But with extenuating circumstances. Authors should be allowed to plead curiosity, like a madman pleads insanity. Same sort of situation. Can't help themselves. So I'll ask again. What was it this Ty was pestering you to do that you didn't want to?"

Rudy shrugged and filled his mouth with pancake

again. While he chewed he thought about Murph's question and possible good answers. There weren't any actually, at least not any that were true. On the one hand there was a part of his mind that could almost wish that Murph had overheard what Barney and Ty were planning, but since he hadn't that was the end of it. He, Rudy Drummond, wasn't going to turn into a fink at this stage of the game, particularly not when finking would mean getting Barney in trouble.

He swallowed and said, "I'm not sure what it was that particular time. Probably he was just talking up some daredevil stunt he wanted to do. Like going down Cliff Road on our skateboards, maybe. Ty likes to do dangerous stuff."

"Dangerous," Murph muttered. "Dangerous hardly describes Cliff Road on a skateboard. Suicidal is more like it." But after Rudy assured him that they weren't going to do the Cliff Road thing he finally changed the subject and quit asking questions. And a little later, when the food was all gone, Rudy said good-bye and thanked Murph and went home—with a lot on his mind.

There were several things he'd been planning to work on that morning, but for some reason he wound up flaked out on the shady side of the veranda. In the big woven rope hammock he sipped a Pepsi and thought about Murph and what he'd guessed, which was pretty amazing, and what he apparently hadn't guessed, or at least not yet.

What Murph had been right about was that he, Rudy, had a big problem and that it had something to do with Barney. But what he didn't know was that the

whole Barnaby Crookshank–Rudy Drummond partner-
ship—or connection, or brotherhood, or whatever you
want to call it—was, just possibly, about to end. And if
it did end it would be because Rudy *was* about to
chicken out on something that was really important to
Barney. Because Rudy was not about to spend the
summer prospecting for gold in the abandoned hard-
rock mine called Pritchard's Hole.

Rudy put one hand up across his face and bit his
lip to shut in something that could have been a lot like
a moan. He didn't think any sound had actually es-
caped, but Ophelia, who had come back from escorting
the M and M's to the baby-sitter, suddenly got up on
her hind legs and snuffled nervously in his ear. Rudy
patted her and pushed her down and went on trying to
cope with the feeling that someone had just dropped a
bowling ball on his midsection, and that a dark tunnel
with a tiny flickering light seemed to be imprinted on
the inside of his eyelids.

Quickly opening his eyes, he tried looking at
something else. Anything to blot out the tunnel thing.
At the sunlight filtering through the leafy limbs of the
dogwood tree, or Murph Woodbury's rusty roof, or
down at Ophelia, who was stretched out beside the
hammock looking up at him anxiously. But none of it
helped. The stomach pain went on and so did the ache
in his throat, which felt as if it had squeezed shut to
hold back something that was pushing to get out.

Stop it, he told himself. *Stop it. Stop it.* Over and
over again until the pain and the crazy panic began to
fade slowly away. Rudy sighed. Obviously he had a
screw loose when it came to certain things and lately it

seemed to be getting worse. Of course, he never had been what you might call fearless when it came to physical-type heroics. But in the past when he started losing it he'd usually managed to put on a good front by joking around or something. But in recent years there had been times when something would happen and all of a sudden he'd hit the panic button in pretty spectacular ways.

Like a couple of years ago when Mrs. Hopper's cocker spaniel had her puppies under the house and she'd insisted that Rudy crawl under to get them out. Or even that time just last December when he'd crawled into the storage area under the stairs to hide some Christmas presents and Moira had locked him in. That kind of silly harmless thing was all it took and suddenly he was in the midst of a full-fledged case of the screaming meemies. And he did mean *screaming.* And now, to make matters a lot worse, in just the last couple of months, the nightmares had started—about the same time Barney and Ty had begun talking up the gold-mining scheme.

It had all started sometime in April when Barney and Rudy arrived at school and Ty was waiting out front for them. After he looked all around as if he thought someone might be trying to spy on them, he started in about this old man he'd met in his dad's real estate office.

"This real old dude named Rooney came in my dad's office yesterday," he whispered, "because he owns some land that he wants to sell. But Dad was busy at the time, so the old guy started talking to me. I was terminally bored at first, but then, when I got the

21

drift of what he was saying, I really began to listen. See, this dude lived in Pyramid Hill when he was young and worked at a mine. Pritchard's Hole, he called it. And he says that he knows for a fact that there's a rich vein of gold in that mine that no one ever knew about except him. And he's dead sure it's still there."

Barney had been enthusiastic right away, but Rudy . . . Well, from the very first moment Rudy hated the idea a lot. He couldn't say why exactly, but he was pretty sure it was all related to the same problem that caused him to hit the panic button about ridiculous things like the crawl space under a house, or the storage closet in his own home. But whatever it was, or wasn't related to, he had known immediately that nothing—not even the sure and certain promise of a million dollars in gold—could make him go down into the old Pritchard mine.

Pritchard's Hole! Murph had told him all about it. The story was that it had been called the Hole by miners who worked there because the owner, Old Man Pritchard, was so stingy he wouldn't put in enough supports to make it into even a halfway safe place to work. So it had always basically been just a big hole in the ground, even back during the years when it was a productive mine. Rudy had seen the boarded-up entrance before, a hodgepodge of rotting wooden posts and planks set into a steep rocky cliff-face out beyond the Catholic cemetery. Picturing that entrance made him shudder and there was no way he was ever going to set foot inside it.

But, of course, that wasn't what he'd told Barney

and Ty. All he said to them was that it couldn't be true about the gold because if it were, lots of other people would know about it and all kinds of prospectors would have been looking for it ages ago.

But Ty had an answer for that too. "But nobody else ever knew about it," he said. "Rooney kept it a secret because he was doing some 'high grading.' High grading?" he repeated, like he didn't think Rudy knew what that meant. "You ever hear of high grading?"

"Sure," Rudy said. He hadn't lived in the gold country all his life for nothing. "That's when a miner sneaks some gold out of a mine where he's a hired worker and keeps it for himself instead of turning it over to the owner."

"Yeah," Ty said. "So this Rooney dude had been sneaking out these big nuggets and he'd already high graded enough stuff to buy himself some land, when he got in a fight at a saloon and almost killed this other dude. So he went to prison and when he got out he didn't dare come back to Pyramid because this dude he'd drilled was out to get him."

"So why doesn't he try to get the gold himself," Rudy asked, "if he's so sure it's still down there?"

"Beats me," Ty said. "Except he's pretty old and crippled. And, of course, he couldn't just go out and hire somebody to get it for him, because, if you want to get technical, it doesn't legally belong to him. All he wanted was to have my dad sell his land and he'd forget about the whole thing, but then, when we got to talking, he decided to let me in on the secret if I'd promise to send him fifty percent or something like that. He even drew me this map that shows exactly where the vein is."

"So we have to send him fifty percent?" Barney asked.

Ty shrugged. "Or something like that. How's he going to know how much we find?"

So then Rudy asked to see the map, but Ty wouldn't show it to him. "Nobody sees the map unless they're in on the project one hundred percent. So—are you in or out, Drummond?"

"I don't know." It all sounded pretty unbelievable, not to mention illegal and dangerous. He reminded Barney about what had been pounded into them by parents and teachers ever since they were born—that nothing in the world was more dangerous than fooling around in an old mine. The whole area around Pyramid Hill was riddled with old mines and every kid who had ever grown up in the gold country knew how dangerous they were. It was the truth, too, not just another adult superstition like don't cross your eyes or they'll stay that way, and don't watch too much TV or your brain will rot. Old mines were full of snakes and spiders, shafts that went straight down forever, flooded passageways, crumbling walls, hidden crevices, and endless, endless . . .

It was starting up again—the pain in his stomach and the feeling that he was about to start screaming—but this time he was able to stop it before it really took over, by using the "think about something else" method. Something great—the greater the better. This time what he thought about was Barney.

Chapter 3

BARNEY. The first time Rudy met Barney was in the kindergarten room at Pyramid Elementary. It wasn't the first day of school, because when the school year started Barney had been away on the rodeo circuit with his parents. By the time he came into the classroom with his grandmother, all the other kids were already feeling like old hands. Mrs. Peters, the teacher, introduced Barney to the class and talked about how glad they all were to meet him, but when Belle Crookshank left, Mrs. Peters went into the hall with her. That left Barney standing all alone up by the chalkboard. Right away the other kids sort of gathered around staring at him to see if he was going to cry—like a lot of them had on their first day.

But Barney didn't cry. He just stood there with his

chin out and with a bunch of his dark-blond hair hanging down over one eye. He didn't look exactly happy, but you got the feeling that he wouldn't have cried if all the kids in the room had suddenly turned into three-headed monsters.

Thinking about monsters gave Rudy an idea. He put his arms straight out in front of him, made a crazy face, and started staggering around the room stiff-legged, bumping into people. When everybody stopped staring at Barney to stare at Rudy he stumbled up to Barney and said, "Hi. I'm Rudy the zombie. Come on, let's zombie." At first Barney just grinned and ducked his head, but by the time the teacher came back into the room everybody was staggering around being zombies, including Barney.

From then on Barney and Rudy played together at school and on weekends and before long Rudy was practically living at the Crooked Bar Ranch.

Maybe Barney and Rudy became good friends so quickly because they were both a little bit lonely. Barney because his parents were away so much of the time, and Rudy because Natasha married Art Mumford right around then and Rudy never felt particularly welcome at home when his stepfather was there. So for about nine years he and Barney had been like brothers, except better because some brothers don't particularly appreciate each other and he and Barney always had.

Of course, Rudy was a long way from being the only Barnaby Crookshank appreciator. Starting from almost his second day in kindergarten Barney was always one of the most popular kids at Pyramid Elementary—being popular was something that Barney never worked at. He was great at every kind of sport, so he always got chosen first for all the teams. And he probably got chosen for other kinds of things because of his looks. Barney had always looked a lot like his father, the rodeo star who was so good-looking that he was known on the circuit as "The Handsome Cowboy." And of course, it didn't hurt Barney's reputation that everyone knew he'd been helping his grandfather at the ranch since he was practically in diapers and at the age of five could have been almost a champion cowboy himself.

One of the things Rudy particularly liked about Barney was how he didn't talk about himself a lot like some popular kids do. In fact, Barney never talked more than necessary about anything, a trait he probably inherited from his grandfather, who was a world-class conservationist when it came to the spoken word. Also, Rudy had always appreciated how Barney never put people down—not even nerds and little kids—like some popular dudes do.

And as for how Barney felt about Rudy—well, for one thing, he'd always seemed to think that Rudy was a major laugh riot. Nobody appreciated Rudy's crazy sense of humor as much as Barney did. For instance, Barney really got a kick out of the "Romeo Rudy" thing. Juliet, of course, was Stephanie Freeman, a girl who'd been in the same class with Rudy and Barney since about second grade.

Even way back then Stephanie was a knockout, with short curly hair and long curly eyelashes and a totally mind-blowing frown. She had a great smile, too, but she didn't use it very often, particularly when

Rudy was around. Her first day at Pyramid happened to be around Valentine's Day, and Rudy had started following her around with a really zonked-out expression on his face, trying to give her a big paper heart he'd made. The rest of the class was used to Rudy and they all thought it was pretty funny—but Stephanie obviously thought he was crazy, which made it all the funnier. After that the whole thing just kept growing.

One time in the cafeteria when they were in third or fourth grade Rudy noticed that no one was eating their raw veggies. So he collected a bunch of celery stalks and carrot sticks and made a kind of bouquet out of them. He got everyone's attention when he went around collecting veggies and especially when he snitched Julie Harmon's hair ribbon to tie the whole thing together. Then, with everyone watching—except for Stephanie, who was determinedly looking the other way—he did a fixing himself up act, slicking down his hair and polishing his shoes on the backs of his pant legs and straightening an imaginary tie. Then he marched down the aisle, went down on one knee with a big flourish and tried to give the bouquet to Stephanie. Everyone cracked up, particularly when she hit him with her lunch pail.

When Rudy did something like that Barney would always say, "How do you have the nerve to do crazy stuff like that?" as soon as he could stop laughing enough to say anything. And Rudy would say something like, "I don't know. Born weird, I guess. You know, kind of . . ." And he'd do a wildman bit, bugging his eyes and panting, with his tongue hanging out the side of his mouth.

28

Perhaps that was another part of the friendship—the fact that Rudy and Barney were, in a lot of ways, about as different as two people could possibly be. Maybe being absolute opposites was one thing that kept them from getting bored with each other.

Things changed some when they were in sixth grade. Barney's grandmother died that year, and at about the same time, Rudy's stepfather decided he wasn't cut out to be a husband and father and went back to Texas. After Art took off Natasha needed Rudy at home, so he had less time to spend at the Crooked Bar. But he and Barney still saw quite a lot of each other and went on being best friends and absolute opposites.

But if being opposites just made their friendship better in most respects, there was one difference that had always been more or less a problem—and that was the thing Barney had about living dangerously. It seemed to Rudy that Barney felt that in order to have a great time, you had to go out and find something to do that stood a pretty good chance of killing somebody, or at least doing them considerable damage. Not many people realized that about Barney because, even though Barney always went first and farthest, the person who got damaged was usually somebody else. Like Rudy, for instance.

There had been the time, for example, when Barney talked Rudy into helping him build a Tarzan-type swing over Wild Horse Gorge. Rudy was pretty sure that it wasn't a red-hot idea, particularly when he stood at the edge of the cliff and looked down at the rocks below. A pain shot up the backs of his legs and something clamped down on his throat, so he had to swallow hard before he could speak.

"Er, look, Barn," he said. "Do you mind if we put this off till tomorrow? I just remembered something I have to do immediately, if not sooner. Like check on my life insurance."

He was trying to make a joke of it, but it didn't work. In fact, Barney hardly seemed to hear him at all. Standing at the edge of the cliff, he stared out across the chasm with unblinking eyes and a tight, excited look on his face. Then without even looking at Rudy he yelled "Geronimo" and swung across to the other side as easy as anything. So Rudy yelled and jumped too—and crashed into the cliff on the other side.

And then there had been tightrope walking in the barn loft, and bucking-horse riding, and high diving from the top of a storage tank into the stock watering trough down below.

There'd been a lot of other such adventures. Some of them Rudy could barely remember, even if he tried to—which wasn't often, because remembering was just too painful, and not just because of the various bruises and lacerations. The most painful part was remembering how world-class chicken he'd usually been and how hard it was to keep it from showing.

Actually, not all of Barney's great ideas had turned out as badly as the Tarzan swing, and some of them Rudy really got pretty good at—after he got over the terror. Usually Barney was very easygoing, but when he started on one of his daredevil schemes he would get a strange look in his eyes—almost like a Jekyll and Hyde thing—and there was just no use arguing. But sometimes Rudy was able to talk him out of the most obviously fatal ones. Or he had been, at least, until Ty Lewis appeared on the scene.

At that point Rudy opened his eyes and came back to the present—the gentle rocking of the hammock and the warm bright air of midmorning. Going back over his friendship with Barney had taken his mind off his problems at least for the present, and he was feeling pretty much back to normal. He was beginning to think about all the things he ought to be doing when he suddenly heard a familiar sound. The clink and whir of approaching bicycles. And then voices—also familiar. Sitting up so quickly that he almost capsized the hammock, he looked up the street and there they were— Barnaby Crookshank and Ty Lewis. Ty Lewis! Ophelia started barking. Rudy knew how she felt.

Chapter 4

RUDY LOOKED AT HIS WATCH. Barney must have started off pretty early to have biked in from the ranch already. And he'd obviously gone straight to Ty's house without even stopping off to see Rudy first. And now the two of them were on their way downtown, and as they passed Rudy's house, laughing and talking, it almost looked as if they weren't even planning to slow down. But when Rudy yelled, "Haybarn!" they skidded to a stop. At least Barney did. Ty went on almost half a block before he braked and circled slowly back.

"Hey, Rudy-dudey." Barney rode out the skid and then jumped off at the last second. He was wearing faded jeans and unlaced L.A. Gear sneakers and his usual wide-angle grin. Leaning his bike against the fence, he jumped over the gate and started up the steps to Rudy's veranda. But Ty didn't. When he finally came to a stop in front of the fence he just yelled, "Yo, dude," and went on sitting on his shiny new twenty-one-speed Klein.

After Barney had grabbed the edge of the hammock and pretended he was going to dump Rudy, they roughhoused for a minute before he sat down on the railing. "Cool it, poodle," he said to Ophelia, who was jumping around and barking her head off.

Ophelia, who, like everybody else, was crazy about Barney, immediately shut up.

"Yeah?" Barney said, making it into a question.

"What's up?" Rudy got out of the hammock. "As in—where are you dudes off to?"

Barney grinned. "Shopping," he said, "and scrounging."

"Yeah, and we're in a hurry," Ty called. "I got to get back home to do some stuff for my dad. Come on, Barn."

"Shopping?" Rudy asked.

"For some stuff we're going to need for—" Barney lifted an eyebrow. "You know."

Rudy knew, all right. "Like what?"

Barney lowered his voice. "Rock picks. And hard hats, if we can find some. Ty thinks he knows where we can get some real miners' helmets. You know, the kind with the light on the top. Want to come along?"

A picture began to flash in Rudy's mind. A faint wavering light . . . an oozing rock wall . . . and beyond that, darkness. . . . It took all his strength to keep from wincing as he said, "Oh, yeah? Where you going to find miners' helmets? I don't think they carry them at K mart."

Barney laughed. "Not K mart. Old Jake's. Ty saw some there."

"Yeah." Ty had given up on getting Barney to leave immediately. He leaned his bike against the fence and was on his way up the steps. "Jake has a bunch of them. In that back room where he has that kind of museum of old mining stuff."

"They're like antiques," Barney broke in, "but Jake has a lot of them and Ty thinks we can fix them up with new . . ." His eyes focused on something out past Rudy's shoulder and his voice trailed off into silence. From the glazed look in Barney's eyes and a moment later in Ty's, too, Rudy guessed what was happening before he turned around and saw her—Heather Hanrahan.

Heather Hanrahan, eighteen years old and terminally gorgeous, had been Rudy's neighbor all his life. It didn't surprise him at all that both Ty and Barney seemed to have gone into shock. Heather had that effect on some people. Like, just about every male in Pyramid. Rudy, himself, could hardly pretend to be immune. It was just that having grown up practically next door to Heather, he'd more or less gradually gotten used to her and . . . He stopped grinning at Barney, glanced back at Heather—and lost his train of thought.

She was dressed in some kind of western riding outfit—high-heeled boots, tight jeans, and a snug plaid shirt open at the neck. The Heather who had once been Rudy's baby-sitter and who had helped him learn how to read had always been good-looking, but this glamorous cowgirl was something else again.

She came closer, awesomely slender and at the same time curvy in her tight outfit. And it wasn't until she looked up toward the veranda and smiled that Rudy got it together enough to say something. He wanted to say something—anything—to make her stop and talk to him. For one thing, it would give him lots of points with Ty and Barney. But there was beginning to be another reason, and even though it was still vague and undeveloped, he already felt it was going to be very important.

Closing his mouth, which must have been hanging open a little, he gulped hard and called, "Hey, Heather. Wait a minute."

She stopped, smiling calmly. She'd always been that way, calm and unflappable and not the kind of person you could put anything over on. Not even when you were a kid and she was your baby-sitter. He'd learned that in a hurry, and after they'd worked that out they gradually developed what you might call a neighborly kind of relationship. The kind of neighbors who enjoy each other's company but who know exactly where the fences are.

Heather had always appreciated Rudy's impersonations, so now he sauntered toward her doing his Windy Dayes bit. A few feet from where Heather stood he paused, hitched up an imaginary gun belt, spraddled his legs and said, "Well, howdy there, ma'am. You fixin' to ride on in to Dodge City?"

She laughed and Rudy gulped. A laughing Heather—even white teeth, red lips, and crinkling long-lashed eyes—was really mind-boggling. Even to an old neighborhood friend like himself. He could just imagine what it was doing to Ty and Barney.

"Not exactly," she said. "I don't think I'm ready for Dodge City yet. Next month maybe."

"Next month?" Rudy asked.

"Yes. After I learn how. I'm taking the beginners riding class at Lawford's. Starting today."

"Oh, yeah? The beginners class? You mean you haven't ridden before?"

"Oh, I've been on a horse once or twice, but not enough to really learn how," Heather said. "My folks never could afford lessons."

That wasn't a surprise. Heather's father had never been able to hold a job for very long because he was sick a lot. But then, Rudy's family had always been even poorer and Rudy had been riding since he was five. But the difference, of course, had been being Barney's friend.

"So now I'm going to learn how," Heather said. "Before I go away to college."

"Yeah. I heard about your inheritance. Pretty neat. Wish I had a rich uncle."

Natasha had told him about the inheritance just last week, after Heather had been over for a visit— Heather and Natasha had always been pretty buddy-buddy. A great uncle, or someone like that, had left Heather some money just in time for her to use it for her college education. So now she was going to be able to go away to Sacramento State in the fall, instead of living at home and going to the local junior college like she had been planning to do.

"Well," Heather said, "it ought to get me through school if I'm careful. *And* pay for riding lessons. I've been absolutely dying to learn to ride for years and years."

At that moment the plan in the back of Rudy's mind took a giant stride forward. He was beginning to see that he might be able to use his "old buddies" relationship with Heather to get certain people's minds off certain other things—like gold mining.

"Look," he said, falling into step as Heather started down Lone Pine. "Why are you taking riding at Lawford's? From what I hear their horses are in pretty bad shape. Like, one foot in the glue factory."

Heather smiled. "Oh, they're not that bad. And the good news is they've got a lot of nice, safe, lazy ones for beginners like me."

"Well, yeah, safe I guess. Unless one dies on you. From what I hear they're dropping like horseflies. Having a dead horse land on you can pretty much ruin your whole day."

Actually, Rudy had never ridden at Lawford Stables, but he'd heard Barney and his granddad talking about how riding-stable horses tended to be worn out from overwork and spoiled by having had so many greenhorn riders who didn't know what they were doing. But his plan was really taking shape now, and part of it was to convince Heather that trying to learn to ride at the Lawford stables was a big mistake.

"Look," he went on. "How would you like to have some riding lessons on a really great horse? For free."

Heather stopped walking. Putting her hands on her hips, she gave Rudy an amused yet exasperated frown and said, "What are you raving about now, Rudy Drummond? You don't have a horse."

"Hey! You're right!" Rudy whacked himself on the forehead, like the problem had just occurred to him. Then he mimed an "I've got it" expression and said, "However, I know someone who does. And I'm sure something could be arranged by Rudolph Drummond, Private Lesson Arranger, First Class."

Heather was looking suspicious, but at the same time a little bit interested. "How about it?" Rudy said. "Free lessons on a great horse. You with me?"

"Look." Heather suddenly looked at her watch. "I've got to run. I'm late." She started off and then turned back. "We'll talk later. If you're not kidding . . ."

"I'm not. I'm not. I'm serious. I'm totally, absolutely . . ."

Heather waved impatiently and started off down the street.

"I'm serious. Totally serious. I couldn't be more serious if . . ." Rudy gradually ran down as he realized that Heather was out of earshot. Watching her departing back, he sighed, and then turned to where Ty and Barney were still waiting on the veranda. As he came up the steps they both stared at him with what was obviously new respect. Especially Tyler.

"Way to go, Rudy-dudey!" Barney said, grinning.

Ty's eyes were still glassy-looking. Punching Rudy in the shoulder, he said, "Hey, Rudy, baby. What's your secret? What were you and the Ice Princess rapping about?"

"The Ice Princess?" Rudy asked.

"Yeah," Barney said. "That's what Ty calls her."

"Oh, yeah? Why?"

Ty only shrugged, but Barney laughed. "Because she really cooled him when he tried to put a move on her."

"I don't believe it," Rudy said to Ty. "I just don't believe it." Where did Ty get the idea that an eighth-grade dude could get away with hitting on a senior in high school? Particularly one like Heather Hanrahan, who had not only been homecoming queen and county fair princess, but who was also a straight A honor student.

Ty ran his hand over his bristly haircut, and with a supercool shrug said, "So she iced me. So what? I thought it was worth a try."

"Worth a try," Rudy said, trying to keep a straight face. "Okaaay. Got it. And next week you're going to take a crack at Princess Di?"

That really broke Barney up. Ty laughed, too, but it was clear that he didn't think it was all that funny. So after a minute or so Rudy cooled it.

"Hey, chill out, Crookshank," he said to Barney, who was still laughing. "I have news with a capital *N*. Wait until I tell you what I was talking about with . . ." He nodded in the direction that Heather had disappeared.

Barney stopped laughing immediately. Rudy waited until he had their complete attention before he said, "How would you two dudes like to give Heather Hanrahan private riding lessons? With my help, of course."

Ty snorted. "Riding lessons? What kind of a hair-ball idea is that? I don't know anything about riding horses." He stopped suddenly and looked at Barney, who was nodding.

"Yeah," Barney said. "Applesauce. Applesauce would be great for a beginner."

"Sure," Rudy said. "She'd be perfect. As long as she doesn't see any barrels."

Ty was looking confused. "Hey, wait a minute. Would you two dweebs mind telling me what language you're speaking?"

Explaining something to Ty made a nice change, because usually he was the big authority on almost anything you'd care to mention. But when it came to the Crooked Bar Ranch and ranches in general, he was totally clueless. He'd been out to the ranch a couple of times with Barney and Rudy, but apparently he hadn't even heard that Barney's parents were rodeo performers—which was, Rudy had to admit, something Barney tended not to mention very often.

"Applesauce is Barney's mom's mare," Rudy said. "She's a barrel racer."

"Barrel racer?" Ty said with his usual scornful snort. "You mean you got horses out there that race with barrels?"

"Not with," Barney said. "Around. The barrels are turnaround points and you have to go around them at top speed."

"A good barrel horse goes around those things practically horizontal," Rudy told Ty. "Like doing a killer wheelie, only on legs instead of wheels. When old Applesauce sees those barrels she really gets hyped. But the rest of the time she's a real cream puff.

She's got a great mouth and she's the smoothest ride this side of a Rolls-Royce. After riding those riding-stable clunkers Heather will think she's died and gone to heaven."

Rudy could tell that Ty was trying not to look impressed. "You do that too?" he asked Barney. "That barrel racing stuff?"

Barney shrugged. "Yeah, I've done it some. But I like roping better. That's what my dad does on the circuit. My dad ropes and bulldogs and he used to ride broncs when he was younger. And my mom does stunt riding and barrel racing."

"No way!" Ty said. "You mean your mom stands up on the horse's back and jumps on and off and that kind of stuff?"

"Yeah," Barney said. "All that kind of stuff."

"You mean your *mom*? The one I met that day out at your place?"

Barney did a slow grin and then said, "Same one. Only one I've got."

"No way," Ty said again.

Rudy had been about to mention that he'd done some barrel racing on Applesauce himself, but then he thought better of it. It probably wouldn't be too smart to make Ty feel that he was going to be the only green-horn or he might back out of the whole project.

As it was, he wasn't too happy about it. "I don't know," Ty said. "I'm not all that stoked about this horse thing. I sure wouldn't mind getting up close and personal with Hanrahan, but as far as the riding thing is concerned—forget it. Horses hate my guts."

Then he went on to tell about how, when he was a

little kid, he'd been really turned on by cowboy stuff. So his folks hired one of those traveling photographers who come to your house and bring a pony. "One of those black-and-white spotted jobs," Ty said. "That horse took one look and decided to dog-meat me. I told my mom so, but she didn't believe me. Sure enough, as soon as they put me on his back that four-legged hit man took off across the lawn and hung me up in the badminton net. The next day I dumped my hat and boots in the garbage and forgot all about growing up to be a cowboy. Haven't been on a horse since. So how am I going to teach someone to ride when I don't know how myself?"

"Barney can teach you first," Rudy said quickly, fighting the grin that was oozing out at the thought of Ty dangling from a badminton net like a fly in a spiderweb. "He taught me."

Ty looked at him, narrow-eyed. "Then you're an expert at this horse stuff, too, Chickie-baby?"

"Hey, Lewis!" Barney said in a threatening tone of voice, and Ty got the message. Barney had warned him to stop calling Rudy "Chicken" or "Chickie," or even "Kentucky Fried," which he seemed to think was particularly funny.

"Okay. Okay. Rudy-baby," Ty said quickly. "You an expert, too, or what?"

Rudy shook his head. "No, not an expert. Not like Barney. But it doesn't take long to learn enough to look pretty good. Barney can give you a lesson or two first, and by the time Heather shows up you can look like an old cowhand. She'll really be impressed."

"Sure. Sure she will," Ty said sarcastically, but a

little later he asked Barney if he could really teach him to ride in a hurry. And before they left he had agreed that, in a day or two, he'd go out to the ranch for his first riding lesson.

The whole discussion had taken up so much time that, when it finally ended, it was too late for the scrounging trip downtown. So getting the miners' helmets was going to have to wait until some other time—which didn't exactly break Rudy's heart.

Chapter 5

AFTER TY AND BARNEY LEFT, Rudy finally got into gear and started in on the things he'd meant to get done that morning—like fixing his bicycle chain, vacuuming the living room—a promise he'd made Natasha—and finishing an almost-overdue library book. The bicycle chain, he decided, had better come first— in case he needed to ride out to the ranch some time soon for Heather's first riding lesson.

After spreading out his tools in the shady spot where the grape arbor crossed the driveway, he started changing the broken links in the chain and thought about what his approach would be the next time he saw Heather.

He felt pretty good about the Heather thing. Actually, it was his third scheme for dealing with the gold-mining problem, and it seemed to be the best one yet. The second, volunteering to baby-sit his sisters, had been a desperate move when his number one plan, to get a job downtown, hadn't worked out.

What he'd been planning to do originally was get a full-time job so that whenever Ty and Barney wanted him to go gold mining he could just say something like, "Wish I could, but I'm on duty at the firehouse at that particular time."

Of course, that wouldn't solve the whole problem —like the part about Barney spending so much time with Ty this summer. Or the part about Barney doing something that was not only dangerous but also illegal. The illegal part was something new. It had only been recently that Barney had found a new kind of dangerous activity to play around with. In the past, Barney's worst schemes had been the kind that might put somebody in the hospital, but since Ty had appeared on the scene there'd been a few that just might have wound up in the police station. Adventures that involved things like graffiti spray-painting, swiping street signs, and jimmying soft-drink machines to get free Cokes.

There didn't seem to be anything Rudy could do about that sort of thing. He'd tried. But like always, lecturing Barney only made him more determined, and gave Ty another reason to go into his "Rudy the chicken" act. So, short of turning into a fink, there was nothing Rudy could do.

But at least having a steady job would give him a better excuse for his personal cop-out. A better excuse than admitting the truth, which was that, where gold mining was concerned, he was a bigger chicken than anyone, even Ty Lewis, could possibly imagine.

So he'd spent a lot of time looking for a job, but when he'd been turned down by the fire department, and the hotel, and the service station, and a half dozen other places, he'd gotten so desperate that he told Natasha he was willing to spend his summer taking care of the M and M's.

At first she couldn't believe he meant it, but that didn't surprise Rudy. It wasn't easy for him to believe either. When she finally did believe him she said it was very noble of him. So noble that she would only agree to having him baby-sit in the afternoons, so he could have his mornings free. That seemed okay. He'd heard Ty say that he usually slept late during vacations, so mornings probably weren't going to be a problem. So it was settled, and there went all his afternoons, except on Natasha's days off.

But when you came right down to it, having to admit you were stuck with a summer of baby-sitting was embarrassing too. To say that you couldn't go gold mining because you had to fight fires was one thing, but to say you had to baby-sit your sisters was something else again. Besides which, it didn't give him any way out at all on Mondays and Tuesdays, which were Natasha's days off. Still, it had been the best plan he could come up with until the Heather thing happened.

The bicycle chain was still in pieces when the M and M's came around the corner. Ophelia ran to meet them and they stopped to play with her for a minute before they noticed Rudy sitting in the driveway and raced each other up to get to him.

"Hi, Rudy," Moira said. "What are you doing?"

"Yeah. What are you doing?" Margot squatted beside him and pushed her curly mop of blond hair right in front of what he was trying to do. "Can we do it too?"

Rudy stifled a sigh, shoved her out of the way, and went on trying to get the chain back on the bicycle. "Look," he said. "I have to get this finished right away."

"Why? Why do you have to?" Margot's head was back in the way. This time Rudy shoved her a little harder and she tipped over on the driveway. Her lower lip turned down and began to wobble.

"Ye gods," Rudy muttered under his breath. A whole summer of stupid questions and whiny complaints. He didn't see how he was going to stand it. He went on fooling with the chain for a minute or two to calm himself down before he said, "Look. Why don't you guys just quit bothering me for just a few more minutes. Why don't you just go play in the backyard or something."

"But Mom said you were going to play with us," Moira whined. Squatting down, she picked up Rudy's pliers and tried to use them to untie Margot's shoelaces. "Mom said you promised."

Rudy grabbed the pliers and put them back in the tool chest. "I will, I will play with you. Just as soon as I finish this." It was about then that the chain pinched his finger and slipped off the sprocket wheel for the third or fourth time. "Get out!" he yelled. "Get out of here before I . . ."

They stared at him, wide-eyed. Margot's chin was

47

trembling again and Moira's face was screwed up as if she expected to be hit. Rudy took a deep breath, counted to ten, and started over.

"Look," he said. "I need a little privacy because, well, at the moment I'm putting rocket blasters on my bicycle so I can shoot right up into the sky. You know, like they did in *E.T.*"

Moira's eyes went from narrow slits to wide and dreamy with amazing suddenness. "Yeah," she said in a breathless voice. "Right up across the moon." Moira was like that. She usually believed all his weird stories even when she knew better. She looked at Margot. "Rudy's going to fly across the moon on his bicycle," she said.

Margot was still frowning. "Can people really do that? On bicycles?" she asked.

"Sure they can," Moira said. "Come on. Let's go in the backyard and play flying bicycles. Okay?"

Rudy couldn't believe his luck. In another fifteen or twenty minutes the chain was back in working order and he put the bicycle in the garage and went into the backyard where the M and M's were still running around in circles holding imaginary handlebars and making flying noises. They were so busy playing that he was able to go into the house and fix himself a sandwich and get the book on supernatural creatures he'd checked out of the library. They were still at it when he came back out, so he sat on the back steps and ate the sandwich, and read about dragons and vampires.

The flying bicycle game turned out to be a real winner. It lasted for almost an hour during which time there was only one brief outbreak of shoving and punching serious enough to force Rudy to interrupt his reading. And then it only took a brief threat—"Okay! The next one to throw a punch is dog meat"—and things settled down enough so that Rudy could go back to his book.

When the bicycle game finally fizzled they went indoors and had cookies and milk and read the funny paper before they really started pestering Rudy to think of something else they could do.

When he said, "Well, you haven't practiced your ballet today," they only glared at him, and when he suggested that they play with their Barbie dolls, they both groaned.

"Barbie dolls are boring," Margot said. "And besides, Mom said you were going to play with us."

Rudy groaned. Thanks a lot, Mom. But he supposed she'd felt she had to say something to make the M and M's accept the new arrangement. They'd always really liked going to Eleanora's and they'd thrown a fit when Natasha told them they would have to start coming home right after lunch. So, of course, she'd told them about all the fun things they could do at home with Rudy.

"All right," Moira said, "then read to us. Mom said you were going to read to us too. How about the Bobbsey Twins?"

Rudy opened his book. "How about supernatural creatures? The next chapter is on werewolves. Okay?"

So they all three—four counting Ophelia—settled down on the saggy old couch in the living room and Rudy read the werewolf chapter. It was another big success. The M and M's were crazy about his werewolf impressions, and even when he was just reading they listened so hard they almost forgot to blink.

When he got to the end of the chapter he had a brainstorm. "Hey," he said. "What if Barbie was at a dance one night and she stayed until midnight and on the way home she started getting these big fangs and fur all over—"

He didn't have to go any further. He hadn't even finished the sentence when they dashed out of the room.

The M and M's played Barbie doll werewolves all the rest of the afternoon and Rudy was able to get some more reading done and do the vacuuming and even spend some time making plans about Heather's riding lessons.

Natasha came home a little bit later than usual. She looked tired and tense, and when Rudy asked how her day had gone she said she'd had another quarrel with her boss and smashed her finger in the antique cash register, and her brand-new panty hose had sprung a gigantic run.

"Other than that, it was lovely," she said. Then she collapsed on the couch and kicked off her shoes and twisted her leg around to look at the run. "Look at that," she said. "Just bought them yesterday. Three eighty-five down the drain."

She was looking pretty depressed and she didn't even laugh when Rudy said, "Hey, how about if we make a lot more runs in them so you can pretend they were meant to be that way. You know, like buckshot jeans. That kind of stuff is really in lately."

All Natasha managed was a weak smile, and then

she sighed, leaned her head back, and closed her eyes. She sat that way for several minutes. Rudy sat down sideways across the overstuffed chair and waited.

With her head tipped back that way and her dark hair kind of smoothed back Natasha looked—well, like a ballet dancer, which is what she was until she gave it up when she was only nineteen and came back home to Pyramid. She'd been pregnant with Rudy at the time, but that wasn't the only reason she'd given up on the dancing. She had, as she'd told Rudy more than once, decided to come home even before she found out she was pregnant, because her mother was very sick and needed her. So she came back to the old house where the Drummond family had lived since soon after the gold rush and took care of her mother, and after his birth, of Rudy too. Then her mother died while Rudy was still a baby and a couple of years later Art Mumford came along and Natasha decided to marry him. Of course, Art didn't last too long as a husband, but by the time he left there were the M and M's and Natasha was pretty much stuck in Pyramid Hill.

Not having a legal father had never bothered Rudy all that much. Natasha said his real father was a really great guy, but that he wasn't the marrying kind and that she didn't blame him for what happened. So Rudy had never particularly blamed him either—although he could see how having a baby when she was so young hadn't made Natasha's life very easy. And marrying Mumford and having the M and M's certainly hadn't helped either.

Rudy was still thinking about all the extra problems Natasha had gotten herself into by marrying

51

Mumford when, right on cue, the sound of squeals and thuds drifted down the hall. Two little Mumford problems heard from. Natasha opened her eyes, looked toward the door, and sighed. "Fighting again," she said. "And again and again, I suppose?"

"No, not really," Rudy said. "Things have been pretty peaceful around here, actually. Only a minor skirmish or two all afternoon." Raising his voice, he called, "Hey, you two, *knock it off.* Mom's home."

The M and M's appeared in the doorway a second or two later looking startled. "Knock what off?" Margot asked, doing a superinnocent thing with her big round eyes.

"You know what," Rudy said. "We heard you."

They stared at each other blankly for a moment before Moira laughed. "Oh, that," she said. "We weren't fighting. We were just killing a werewolf."

Natasha looked puzzled, but when Rudy grinned and said, "Oh well, that's perfectly all right, then," she finally smiled too. She held out her arms and the M and M's ran to hug her. They were all three curled up on the couch together and the M and M's were chattering away about how good they'd been and how they hadn't had any fights, and Natasha was laughing and chattering, too, when Rudy struggled out of the saggy old chair and wandered into the kitchen.

While he was staring into the refrigerator and hoping that Natasha had something planned for dinner he could still hear the three of them giggling back in the living room. Natasha was like that—up one minute and down the next. Rudy had always figured that being a ballet dancer had something to do with it.

Chapter 6

RUDY HAD PLANNED to phone Heather the next morning, but when he was out on the veranda seeing the M and M's off to the sitter he happened to glance down toward the Hanrahans and there she was in her front yard. So he decided to drop by for an in-person talk instead. It was an especially hot morning and Heather, who was watering the rose bushes, was wearing short shorts and a tank top. Rudy really had to concentrate to keep his mind on what he'd planned to say.

"Well, how bad was it?" he asked as soon as they'd both said hello.

"How bad? Oh, you mean the riding lesson. You were right, I guess. About riding-stable lessons being pretty awful. We spent most of the hour learning how to mount and dismount." She sighed. "I heard it so many times I know it by heart. Let's see. 'Mount from the left of the horse. Hold the saddle horn and the reins in your left hand. Turn the stirrup with your right hand and put your left foot into it. Swing around and up.' "

"Yeah," Rudy said. "That's pretty much what Charlie says. You know, Barney's granddad. I mean, he wanted you to have control of the reins while you're getting on. But how come you had to do it so many times?"

Heather laughed and shrugged. "Well, there were some special problems in the class. Like a bunch of very little kids and two very big women. Okay—fat, actually. Every time we mounted, each of the little kids needed a booster person, and the fat ladies needed two. There were only the two instructors, so it turned out to be a fairly time-consuming process. Then the instructors insisted that we all had to keep doing it until everyone had it right."

"And the horses just stood still and let them get on and off all those times?" Rudy asked. "Some horses get kind of impatient when you do stuff like that."

Heather grinned. "Well, I'm afraid you were right about riding-stable horses. Most of them seemed perfectly happy just to stand still. It's just when you try to get them to do something else that you run into problems."

"Yeah," Rudy said. "So I hear. But just wait till I tell you about Applesauce."

"You're going to tell me about applesauce?" Heather's frown was almost as mind-boggling as her smile. "What are you raving about now, Rudy Drummond?"

So he told her. About how Applesauce was a part Arabian that belonged to the Crookshanks. A dapple-gray mare with a long wavy mane and tail, and very lively and full of energy without being a bit hard to handle. He knew he was doing a good job, because when he finally ran down Heather's eyes had a glassy out-of-focus look and she sighed wistfully before she said, "But are you sure it's all right with Barney?"

"Absolutely," Rudy told her.

Heather sighed again, turned off the water, and dried her wet hands on her shorts . . . and for a moment Rudy lost track of what she was saying. Almost everything Heather did seemed to have that kind of effect on him lately. "Rudy. Are you listening to me? How about his parents?" she was saying when he tuned back in. "Don't they care if he uses their valuable horses to give lessons to beginners? You sure this isn't just another one of your crazy ideas, Rudy?"

"Look," he said, "I'll have Barney call you himself and tell you it's all right. Okay?"

Heather seemed to like that idea, so as soon as he got home Rudy called up Barney and told him that Heather wanted to talk to him.

There was a long pause before Barney said, "You mean you want me to call her up?"

"Yeah. That's what I said. Weren't you listening?"

"Me? Call up Heather Hanrahan? On the phone?"

Rudy chuckled. "Yeah. You want me to tell you how it's done? First you pick up the receiver and—"

55

"Knock it off, Drummond," Barney said. "I just mean . . . I don't think she'll talk to me."

"Of course she will. She *said* she wanted you to call and tell her if it was all right. Why wouldn't she talk to you?"

"Well, I don't know. It's just that—well, I was with Ty that time he tried to get funny with her and I think she blamed me too. She told us both to get lost and stay lost. So I don't know if . . ." Barney's voice trailed off.

Rudy was puzzled. It just didn't sound like Barney Crookshank. Not old Easy-knees Barney, who was always so superrelaxed in any kind of situation, even when girls were around. Not that he said all that much to girls—but being Barney, he didn't have to. When girls were around Barney they tended to do all the talking necessary—not to mention giggling and flirting —so all he had to do was stand there looking cool. Barney had always been a natural at *cool,* but at the moment he didn't sound that way at all.

"Look, Barn," Rudy said. "I promise that she said she wanted you to call. And all you have to do is tell her it's all right with you and your folks if she rides Applesauce. Oh, and Barney. Be sure to make the lesson early in the morning or else on a Monday or Tuesday. Otherwise I can't be there."

"Okay," Barney said. "Okay. I'll tell her Monday or Tuesday. And you'll come too? Okay? You be sure to be here."

"Okay," Rudy said, and then he hung up and just sat there wondering what in the world had gotten into Barney. But later in the day Barney called back, sounding more like himself, and said it was all arranged and Heather's first lesson was scheduled for Tuesday, because Barney had promised to give Ty Lewis a crash course in cowboying on Monday.

Ty's first lesson was something Rudy didn't want to miss, although he wasn't too sure how he wanted it to turn out. The thing was, he wanted Ty to like horseback riding well enough that he wouldn't start pressuring Barney to forget about the whole thing and go back to concentrating on gold mining. But at the same time he couldn't help hoping that Ty didn't exactly turn out to be a natural-born cowboy. Anyway, he was really curious to see how it would go.

On Monday morning he got out his rickety old bike and rode out to the Crooked Bar Ranch right after breakfast.

The house and most of the other ranch buildings at the Crooked Bar were set in the middle of a wide valley. On each side grassy hills swept upward to where stands of pine and oak made green splashes on the smooth golden slopes. On the road that curved down from the highway you got only occasional glimpses of buildings and fences until you turned a corner and there it was spread out just below—a typical cattle ranch right out of *Gunsmoke* or an old John Wayne movie. On the left was the long, low ranch house surrounded by shade trees and a high hedge. Then came the big open barnyard with a hay barn and some sheds off to one side. And farther over to the right were the stock barn, several corrals, and a big practice arena.

Rudy always got a charge out of that first sight of the Crooked Bar. And the smell of it too—a kind of dusty western perfume made up of mixed parts of piney hills and grassy fields, with a subtle hint of horse and cow. He sniffed appreciatively as he pedaled across the cattle guard and headed down the long drive. It was a smell that always seemed to bring back a lot of good memories: when Barney had seemed like a brother and Belle and Charlie Crookshank had seemed very much like his own grandparents. There had been a lot of good times during those years and the sight and smell of the valley always brought it all back.

Applesauce was already tied to the hitching rail outside the tack room when Rudy pedaled around the end of the hedge and into the barnyard. He was getting off his bike when Barney came out of the barn leading Dynamo, a big bay cow pony that belonged to his dad.

"Hey, Rudy-dudey," Barney said. "What're you doing here?"

"What do you mean, what am I doing here? I said I'd come help with the riding lessons."

"Oh, yeah. I thought you just meant tomorrow when Heather's here. Today it's just old Styler." (Styler was one of Ty's nicknames because of the fact that he was always wearing the latest stuff.) "But that's great," Barney went on. "Old Styler can probably use all the help he can get." He threw Rudy a currycomb and brush. "Here. Make yourself useful while I get the tack."

Rudy started grooming Applesauce and Barney disappeared into the tack room. When he came out carrying bridles and saddle blankets he said, "I'm going to start him out in the arena. But after he's got the hang of it I thought we'd go up the trail a ways toward the high pasture. Why don't you come too. On Bluebell —or else Badger.''

Rudy thought about it and decided on Badger, a big eager-beaver sorrel that he'd ridden quite a lot before. Actually Bluebell, who had smoother gaits, was a better ride, but Badger with his head-tossing high-stepping ways was more—well, more impressive.

He was leading the sorrel out of the barn when Ty's father's big Mercedes roared into the yard in a cloud of dust and skidded to a stop. Ty got out—wearing buckshot jeans with holes in all the right places *and* new black-and-red cowboy boots. As the Mercedes spun in a tight circle and then trailed its dust cloud back toward the cattle guard, Ty sauntered across to the barn, running his comb through his spiky hair.

Barney gave Rudy one of his silent comments—a raised eyebrow and a quick twitch at one corner of his mouth. Barney and his granddad were both experts at silent comments. Then he went on tightening the cinch on Applesauce.

"Yo, dudes." Ty came to a stop a few yards away.

Barney shook the saddle to be sure it was secure before he turned around. "Hey, Styler," he said, and then, cocking his head toward the dust cloud that was still settling down over the yard, "Nice wheelie."

Ty shrugged. "Yeah, my dad, the hot-rodder. The thing is, he's not exactly a happy camper at the moment. I overslept a little, so I had to get him to drive me. He harshed on me all the way out here. But, as you noticed, I did get delivered, C.O.D. Right to the door-step." He grinned. "I've got him pretty well trained, actually."

"Tell me about it," Rudy said, pointing to the new boots. "Guess he sprung for those boots too. Pretty awesome. Those puppies must have set him back two or three hundred."

Ty shrugged and grinned, and circling the horses at a respectful distance, sat down on the edge of the cement water trough.

"So, which one is Applesauce?"

When Barney told him he nodded and then just sat there for a while watching as Barney and Rudy went on with the saddling up. His only comment was when Barney won the minor battle it always took to get Dynamo to open his mouth and accept the bit.

"Way to go," he said. "Crookshank ten—horse zero."

Then he got up and walked around the edge of the horse trough, balancing like a tightrope walker. He didn't get down off the edge of the trough until all three horses were saddled and ready.

When they were inside the corral Rudy got up on Badger and watched while Barney started showing Ty how to mount. At first Ty just watched from a distance and kept asking Barney to demonstrate everything over and over again. When he finally agreed to try it himself he kept glancing over at Applesauce's head as if he were afraid she might turn around and bite him. Watching cool, slick old Styler fidgeting around, with his normally half-mast eyes wide open, it occurred to Rudy that maybe panic buttons were pretty evenly distributed after all. He smiled, wondering what Ty's nightmares were. Like maybe he woke up screaming that he was being attacked by the Shetland Pony from Hell.

Rudy's smile turned into a chuckle, but he didn't say anything. Instead, when Ty was finally in the saddle, he just settled the prancing Badger down to a slow walk and rode beside Ty, telling him how great he was doing and how "he looked to have a natural seat and good hands." Which was a comment that Barney's granddad had made about Rudy when he was beginning to ride.

After Ty had learned a few things about reining and keeping his heels down and his weight in his feet, they practiced walking and then trotting in figure eights. And Rudy went on making encouraging comments even though old Styler's trotting form looked a lot like a bag of potatoes on a trampoline.

"Hey, dude," Rudy said when Ty bounced and flapped back around the ring for the third or fourth time. "You are one all-time natural at this cowboy bit. Isn't he, Barn?"

Barney grinned and said, "Sure he is," in a way that Rudy knew meant just the opposite, but Ty didn't notice. His usual cocky grin was back in place and you could see that he was getting a kick out of the way Applesauce obeyed the slightest touch of the reins. Applesauce was good at making any rider feel like an expert.

By the time they left the corral and started off up the trail, Ty had turned into an old cowhand from the Rio Grande—at least in his own mind. On the trail they did some trotting and even a slow, easy gallop and Ty was getting cockier by the minute. But when they were halfway up to the high valley, Barney suggested they'd better head for home.

"Go back?" Ty said. "No way. I'm just getting the hang of this galloping stuff. I mean like, surf's up, let's hang ten."

He thumped Applesauce with his heels and set off up the trail, bouncing and flapping. Barney did his eyebrow thing at Rudy and then galloped after Ty, grabbed the reins, pulled Applesauce to a stop, and then headed her toward home.

"Hey. What are you doing?" Ty said. "I told you. I don't need to stop. I'm doing great."

But Barney kept hold of Applesauce's reins. "Look, Styler," he said. "You may not feel it now, but wait till tomorrow. You ride three or four more hours today and you won't be able to get out of bed in the morning."

"Not me," Tyler said. "Don't worry about me. People who get stiff when they start riding probably aren't in very good shape to begin with. I mean, somebody who jogs and skies and surfs isn't going to get drilled by loafing around on a horse's back for an hour or two."

But Barney just grinned and kept on leading Applesauce back toward the ranch. When he finally turned her loose Tyler jerked the reins, kicked Applesauce in the ribs, and galloped on ahead toward the barn.

Rudy rolled his eyes at Barney. "Can't wait to see the great cowboy tomorrow," he said, and Barney laughed. But Rudy was careful not to say anything discouraging to Ty.

Let him think he's the world's greatest natural-born horseman, he told himself. *It suits me just fine. Let him be so crazy about being a cowboy he forgets all about being a gold miner. Please, please, please let him forget all about that.*

Chapter 7

THAT NIGHT AFTER DINNER Rudy went out to sit on the veranda. Inside the house the beat-up old dishwasher was rumbling and clattering, the M and M's were yelling at each other, and in the dance studio (ex-dining room) Natasha was doing her ballet exercises to a tape of the *Golliwog's Cakewalk* turned up high to drown out all the other noise. The uproar was pretty deafening, but it didn't bother Rudy all that much. He was used to it, and besides, he was feeling good—a little more optimistic about the summer than he had been for quite a while.

Across the foothills the sun was going down in an awesome red-gold sea of clouds. Kicking back on the old plastic chaise longue that Natasha used for suntanning, Rudy watched until the fiery sky cooled to

gray. Then he sat up and looked around. He felt rest-
less in a good sort of way. Almost like something
needed celebrating.

He knew that nothing was for certain. Heather
could change her mind and back out on the riding lessons or at any time Barney and Ty could lose interest
in the whole riding school project and go back to gold
mining. But the celebration feeling was still there.
Maybe he'd call up Barney to see if he wanted to go
downtown.

During previous summer vacations he and Barney
had met downtown at least a couple of evenings a
week. There were always people they knew there and,
usually in the summer, something special was going
on for the tourist trade. Meeting Barney downtown
was exactly what he felt like doing.

Back in the house he made his way through the
living room to a loud chorus of "Yes, you dids" and
"No, I didn'ts," and through the dining room to the
beat of the *Golliwog's Cakewalk.* In the kitchen the
dishwasher had reached its quieter drying phase, so
the noise level wasn't too bad. Rudy dialed the
Crooked Bar's number and Angela Crookshank, Barney's mom, answered the phone.

"Rudy?" she said in her cool, faraway voice that
always made Rudy think she might have forgotten who
he was. "Barney?" There was a pause—like maybe
she'd forgotten who Barney was too. "Oh, yes. He must
be around here somewhere. Just a minute."

It was quite a while before Barney came to the
phone. At first they talked about Ty and the riding lesson.

"He sure turned into one killer cowboy in a hurry, didn't he?" Rudy said.

"Well." There was a pause and Rudy could picture Barney's raised eyebrow and one sided twitch of a smile. "Well, I guess you could call it that. He's got a ways to go yet, but one thing's for sure. He got over being so freaked out about the whole thing."

"Yeah," Rudy agreed. "Tell me about it. And how about those boots? I've seen boots like that down at Raleighs—with that inlaid leather stuff. I wasn't kidding when I said three hundred dollars. That's what they cost."

"Yeah," Barney said, "or more. Hey, what's up?"

So Rudy asked him if he wanted to go downtown. There was a long pause before Barney answered, and when he did it was obvious he wasn't too enthusiastic. "What's the matter?" Rudy said. "You always liked to hang out downtown."

There was another pause before Barney said, "Well, I'd like to, but I'm cleaning up the tack right now. You know, saddle soaping and stuff like that."

"Oh, yeah? Well, couldn't you do that some other time?"

"Naw. I don't think so. I've got all the cleaning stuff out and if I quit now I'd have to put it all away and start over again later."

Rudy stared at the phone as if he might find some answers printed on the touch-tone buttons. Answers to questions like, Was Barney really that busy or was he just trying to get out of hanging out with an old friend? Instead of a new one, maybe? Rudy was beginning to feel angry, when all of a sudden it came to him what it really was—Heather Hanrahan. Heather was going to be at the Crooked Bar tomorrow and Barney had to have everything just right for her visit. All the tack had to be cleaned and polished, the floor of the horse barn probably had to be swept, and poor old Applesauce was going to get groomed to within an inch of her life.

"Oh, I get it," Rudy said. "It's because Heather's—"

"No." Barney broke in. "That has nothing to do with it. My dad's been after me to clean up the tack for a long time. I just decided tonight would be a good time to do it. Okay?"

"Oh, sure," Rudy said in what must have been a slightly sarcastic tone of voice.

Barney sounded a little angry when he said, "Well, it's the truth."

"Okay, okay." Rudy tried to sound sincere. "I believe you." And then under his breath he added, "And I also believe in the tooth fairy and the Easter bunny."

So Barney said good-bye and no doubt went back to polishing everything on the ranch that Heather might possibly lay eyes on. Which was great actually, when you came to think about it. Nothing could be better than the news that Barney was so wrapped up in Heather's riding lesson that he couldn't think of anything else.

Rudy found that his good mood had returned, so he told Natasha he'd be back in an hour or so and went downtown by himself.

It was a clear, warmish night, and a full moon was hanging over Main Street like a great big outdoor chandelier. In the mingled moon- and lamplight the old wooden buildings with their gingerbread trim and overhanging balconies looked almost as good in real life as they did on the postcards the tourists sent home to Buffalo—or wherever. *Picturesque Pyramid Hill in the Heart of the Sierra Gold Country.*

In fact, everything—not only the buildings, but also the trees, flower boxes, window decorations, and even the local inhabitants—looked mysteriously different, as if seen through a magical veil that somehow smoothed out all the smears and cracks and wrinkles. The people, particularly, seemed strangely changed for the better.

There were quite a few people out and about. Not as many as on weekends, of course, when the whole town swarmed with tourists. But tonight some high school kids with guitars were playing and singing in the little park by the city hall, and a bunch of local types were listening, or going in and out of the bar and restaurant at the Grand Hotel. Rudy knew most of them, and for some reason, maybe because he was feeling good or else because of the moonlight, they all looked a lot better than usual.

Hank Edwards, the mechanic who had saved Betsy the station wagon from the junkyard five or six times, went by looking a little less greasy than usual. And then came Sharon Booker, who had been a good friend of Natasha's since they were in school together, and whose peroxide-blond hair, in the moonlight, looked almost natural. And the Wilson Fairweather family—all ten of them, and all smiling for once. And old Mrs. Hopper and her fat cocker spaniel, who waddled slowly past without smiling, but without whining either, which was possibly a first for both of them.

In front of the library he ran into three girls he'd been in school with for most of his life—Julie Harmon, Jennie Street, and last but not least, Stephanie Freeman. As the three girls came around the corner Rudy did an elaborate double take, staggered back against a lamppost, and slithered down to a sitting position, clutching his chest.

"Arrrgh!" he groaned.

Jennie and Julie laughed hysterically, but Stephanie only frowned and looked the other way. Stephanie Freeman, about whom Rudy had invented his big Romeo number way back in second grade, had lots of great qualities. Her brain, for instance—she was an A student in everything, particularly math and science. Not to mention her face and figure. But she did have one or two little character flaws—like not much personality and absolutely no sense of humor.

Stephanie almost never laughed at anything Rudy did—not even his weekly current events report, for which he was practically famous. In the fourth grade he'd started winding up his current events reports with something like, "And now, a back to the future news flash from the year 2001—the famous movie and television comedian, Rudy Drummond, has just announced his engagement to his beautiful childhood sweetheart, Stephanie Freeman." It got so everybody, even the teacher, sort of counted on Rudy ending up his current events with something about Stephanie. And everyone always fell out laughing—everyone, that is, except Stephanie.

But Rudy had never held Stephanie's personality against her. After all, nobody's perfect, and in other areas Stephanie came closer than most. And, he had to admit, part of the reason his Romeo act had been such a big hit all these years was because Stephanie hated it so much.

Rudy was still collapsed against the lamppost when Jennie squatted down and pretended to take his pulse. "I think he's dying," she said. "Call an ambulance."

Rudy opened one eye and then staggered to his feet. "Never mind," he said, dusting himself off. "It's nothing serious. Only a minor heart attack. I think a Coke at the Parlor would fix me up fine. Anybody for a Coke?"

Stephanie in the moonlight was even more gorgeous than usual, and she actually spoke to Rudy, or at least more or less in his direction. "I can't," she said. "I promised I'd be home by nine."

"Me either," Julie said. "Maybe next time."

"Next time?" Rudy said to Stephanie. "Okay?"

Stephanie almost smiled and said, "Okay," and then she turned around and waved as the three girls started off down Main Street. Rudy waved back, feeling good. With Stephanie a wave and a halfway smile would have to be called real progress.

Still in the mood to celebrate, Rudy went on around town, stopping to talk to people he knew. There were a lot of them. Lots of people and dogs and cats, too, whom Rudy had known for years and years. Everybody said hello—all the people, anyway—and quite a few of them stopped to talk for a minute, including one of Pyramid Hill's most famous characters, old Windy Dayes.

As usual, Windy was hanging out in front of city hall on the lookout for someone who might listen to one of his stories about the old days in Pyramid Hill—and then maybe treat him to a drink in the Grand Hotel bar.

"Howdy there, pardner," Rudy said, sticking out his hand, and Windy howdied back, grinning widely—changing the direction of the wrinkle gullies that ran down his cheeks and showing glimpses of stubby teeth through his straggly mustache.

"Now, don't tell me," he said. "It's old Bill Drummond's grandson—er, don't tell me—your calling name is right thar on the tip end of my tongue."

Windy always remembered Rudy's grandfather's name, and sometimes his mother's, but he usually had a problem with Rudy's.

"Rudy," Rudy said finally. "Rudolph William Drummond."

"Shore it is," Windy said, slapping his thigh and nodding. "Rudy Drummond." He went on nodding for a while before he said, "It's Rudy Drummond and—" He glanced around. "Whar's your sidekick? Good-lookin' young feller with all that yeller hair."

"Barney," Rudy said. Rudy was glad to see that Windy, for one, hadn't forgotten that Rudy and Barney were "sidekicks." "Barney couldn't come to town tonight. He had some work he—"

But Windy had spotted some promising-looking tourists who'd stopped to read the historical marker in front of city hall and he was edging away. He went over to them and Rudy heard him say, "Howdy, folks. Right glad to see you reading up on this here town's history. Mighty historical place, Pyramid Hill. You ever hear tell of . . ."

Rudy moved on—bowlegged, elbows flapping— practicing his Windy Dayes bit on the next two or three people he met, and they all laughed and "how- died" back—knowing he was impersonating Windy, and knowing his reputation as an impersonator too.

It was like that when you'd lived in Pyramid Hill all your life. It wasn't a bad place to grow up, actually. There was something satisfying about knowing so many people whose parents and grandparents, and even great grandparents, had all known each other.

It was just about then that Rudy noticed a familiar- looking couple coming out of the restaurant of the Grand Hotel. The man was tall and square-jawed and the woman was short and plumpish and they were both wearing the style of clothes that Murph called "Hollywood Cowboy." It was the Lewises, Ty's par- ents. They'd met Rudy before, at the eighth-grade grad- uation just the other night, and before that when Ty had taken Rudy and Barney to their brand-new phony Victorian house—which was full of expensive an- tiques, phony and otherwise. Having a mother who worked in an antique store had made Rudy more or less an authority—and he knew a phony antique when he saw one. He'd gotten a good look at all the antiques at the Lewises', and the Lewises had certainly gotten a good look at him. But now they walked right past without recognizing him. He didn't bother to remind them, but a minute later the restaurant door opened again, and an all-too familiar voice said, "Hey, chickie-baby."

It was Ty, all right, wearing a different pair of stylishly shredded jeans, the same flashy red-and-black boots, and carrying a big paper bag.

"Hey, Styler," Rudy said. "What's up?"

"Not much," Ty said. "I've just been doing the town with my old man and lady. They're not much fun, but the good news is—they're loaded. I mean, we're talking b-i-g bucks."

Rudy thought of saying, "Yeah, so you keep saying," but he decided on "Yeah, so I've heard." And then, because the topic of how rich Ty's parents were had been pretty well covered, he changed the subject. "What's in the bag?" he asked. But almost before he finished saying it something told him he didn't want to know.

"I got one," Ty whispered, rolling his eyes to indicate that he was saying something very important. "I told my mom I was starting a collection of antique gold-country stuff, and she fell for it. She's really been into gold-country antiques lately. Look."

He glanced at his parents, who had stopped to look in a window, and then opened the top of the paper bag. Inside was an old beat-up miner's helmet with a carbide lamp on the top.

"I couldn't get her to buy two of them, so Barney's going to have to get his own." He glanced sideways at Rudy. "And you are too. That is, if you aren't going to chicken out on the action."

"Chickening out has nothing to do—" Rudy had

started to say, but Ty was already hurrying after his parents.

On his way home a few minutes later, Rudy made himself walk slowly and concentrate on noticing things like the sound of distant music and the smell of honeysuckle in the cool night air. But it wasn't easy. His good mood had pretty much vanished, and the moon had definitely gone behind a cloud.

Rudy had trouble getting to sleep that night, and when he finally did drop off he had another nightmare. Not about dark tunnels this time, but one almost as scary. He dreamed he had just come home from the store carrying a bag of groceries, but when he put the bag down on the kitchen table he suddenly began to hear the kind of music they play in a movie when something gruesome is about to happen—like when somebody is about to have an intimate meeting with a vampire or get slimed over and digested by the Blob. In his dream he was really scared when he heard the music without knowing exactly why. He looked all around the room and out all the windows, but he didn't see anything, so finally he went back and opened the bag to take out the groceries. But when he looked inside, the milk and bananas had disappeared and all that was in the bag was a miner's helmet. Just an old miner's helmet, but while he was staring at it he kept feeling more and more panicky until he suddenly woke up with his heart pounding and a painful tightness in his throat.

That was all there was to the dream, but the next morning while he was getting dressed he was still thinking about it and hearing echoes of the threatening music. The whole thing definitely felt like some kind of a warning.

He was on his way to the kitchen when the phone rang. He made his usual mad dash to get it, but by the time he got to the kitchen Natasha had picked it up and was talking to someone. Or listening mostly, in between making comments like "Oh no," and "How disappointing." He wasn't paying much attention until he heard Natasha say, "But that really wasn't fair. After all, you paid for a riding lesson, not to sit around and watch people being boosted into the saddle."

"Is that Heather?" he asked.

"Yes. Yes. Well, good-bye dear. Here's Rudy," Natasha said into the phone and then to Rudy, "Here. It's Heather. For you."

He knew it. Heather was calling to back out of the riding lesson. He had just known something terrible was about to happen.

"Rudy." Heather's voice was as great as the rest of her. "I just flashed on something. You might as well ride out to the ranch with me. I'm driving my new car. I'll pick you up at ten o'clock. Okay?"

"Sure," Rudy said very calmly. "Okay by me"— while on the inside he was yelling "Great! Wonderful!" To arrive with Heather at the Crooked Bar, with both Ty and Barney watching! To be seen getting out of Heather Hanrahan's car! Absolutely awesome. The only thing, in fact, that could possibly make it any better would be if he could be the one driving. Which, to be honest with himself, wasn't likely, since he hadn't learned to drive yet, and there probably wasn't time to learn before ten o'clock.

By a little after nine o'clock Rudy had polished his boots, combed his hair four or five times, and even splashed himself with a little of the masculine-type cologne that had been on the top shelf of the medicine cabinet since his stepfather forgot it when he took off for Texas. When he'd done everything he could think of to get ready he paced around the room, looking out the window from time to time. After a while he noticed that Natasha, who had moved into the living room with her coffee and paper, was watching him.

"Now, what is it that you're doing today at the ranch?" she asked finally, in the offhand way she always had when she was particularly curious. "That is, if you don't mind letting your mother in on the secret."

"No secret," Rudy said. "I'm just going to teach Heather to ride. That is, I'm going to help. Actually, Barney and Ty and I are all going to teach her."

"Oh, I see." Natasha's lips were twitching.

"Okay. What are you laughing at now?"

"Oh, nothing. Just wondering how that was going to work. Are you all going to give instructions in unison, or take turns? I can't quite picture it."

"Very funny," Rudy said sarcastically, but then he smiled. "Hey, what's to understand? You've heard of team teaching, haven't you?" Just at that moment a horn honked in front of the house, and without waiting for an answer, he made a mad dash out the door.

Heather was wearing the same awesomely sexy cowgirl outfit she'd worn on Saturday, and her new car wasn't even secondhand. A Toyota, silver-gray, and factory-fresh.

"Hey!" Rudy said when he got in. "Some wheels."

"Well." Heather shifted gears and pulled away from the curb. "It's not a BMW. But it is new. The first new car ever in my family."

"Tell me about it," Rudy said. "All we've ever had is Betsy, at least as far as I can remember. According to my mom, Betsy is like part of the family and a valuable antique besides. Very high-class car. Even runs once in a while." He looked around, running his hands over the sleek upholstery and checking out all the stuff on the dashboard. "But I'd take a new Toyota any day. Remind me to look into this rich uncle bit. I must have one stashed away somewhere."

On the way out to the ranch they talked at first about the car and how Heather's inheritance from her uncle had made it possible. And then they got onto the riding lesson and that brought up the subject of Tyler Lewis.

"Is that Lewis kid going to be there?" she asked.

Rudy couldn't help liking her tone of voice, because it seemed to be expressing some of the same feelings he had about Ty from time to time. Like disgust and hatred. He wanted to say as much, but he knew it wouldn't be a good idea to turn her against Ty any more than she already was. So he just said, "Yes. He'll probably be there."

Heather shrugged. "I was afraid of that. I don't see why you and Barney hang out with that mouthy little creep."

Rudy squelched another grin. "Oh, old Styler— that's what we call him, Styler—Styler's not so bad. Sometimes. And Barney likes him, I guess."

"Yes, so it seems." They were at the turnoff onto the ranch road by then and for a minute Heather was busy with the car, stopping to wait for oncoming traffic, and then shifting gears and turning expertly onto the narrow road. And Rudy was busy watching her. So busy, in fact, he forgot to listen to what she was saying. He got his mind back in gear in time to hear ". . . a bad influence on Barney. He used to be such a great little kid. But now, when I try to talk to him, he just stands around and stares at me."

"Oh, that," Rudy said quickly. "That's just . . ." He paused and thought of saying, "That's just because he's madly in love with you," but decided against it. Instead he said, "That's, well, it's not because Barney's unfriendly or anything. He's just a little shy, I guess."

"That's strange. He didn't used to be shy at all. You know, like back when you two used to play together so much. He didn't seem at all shy then."

Rudy was trying to explain why certain people might become shy at certain times and with certain people even when they weren't shy at all most of the time, when they drove into the ranch. And, sure enough, just as he had hoped, Ty and Barney were both there in front of the horse barn where they couldn't help but see the grand arrival. They couldn't help seeing, for instance, how Rudy jumped out of the car and opened the door for Heather and pointed out things for her as they walked across the barnyard. He pointed out the stock barn and the hay barn and the corrals and the cattle-loading chutes, and Heather listened and nodded.

"And this," he said as they reached the hitching rack. "This—*tah dah*—is Applesauce."

"Oh," Heather said. "Oh, wow!" She stopped walking and just looked, and a supersleek and shiny Applesauce turned and looked back, nodding her beautiful Arab head gently as if to say hello. "Oh, wow!" Heather said again, and then she did her mind-boggling smile—at Applesauce first, and then right at Rudy.

He gulped and went brain-dead. But after a second or two he got it together enough to check to see if Ty and Barney had noticed. They had. The day had definitely gotten off to a good start.

Chapter 8

AFTER EVERYONE SAID "HI"—or "yo," in Ty's case —it looked for a while like the riding lesson was going to bog down. Barney seemed to be doing a bashful hill-billy imitation, shuffling around and staring at the toes of his boots. Ty would start to say something, and then glance at Barney and stop—as if Barney had threat-ened to really drill him if he mouthed off again around Heather, and maybe he didn't know any other way to talk to girls.

Things were about to get embarrassing when Rudy took over and started the ball rolling. Hitching up his pants and doing his weather-beaten old cowhand squint, he looked up at the sun and said, "Waal now, pardners, it's goin' to be high noon afore long. How about if we mosey on over to the OK Corral and get goin'."

"Yeah. Okay. Let's go," Barney said, looking relieved. He untied Applesauce and led her into the arena and the rest of them followed. And after a little more stammering and shuffling around he finally began to tell Heather how to get on and off a horse.

Heather groaned. "Not again," she said. They all laughed when she described her washout of a riding lesson at Lawford's, and after that Barney seemed to loosen up a little.

"So," Rudy said. "Let's see you do it."

So she did, taking the reins in her left hand and then swinging up, as smooth and easy as if she'd been riding all her life. And when Barney began telling her about neck reining she caught on to that real fast too.

When Heather began to ride around the ring, Ty and Barney and Rudy climbed up and sat on the top rail of the fence. Every time she went past, Barney or Rudy told her what she was doing right or wrong and what she ought to try next. Applesauce was her usual sweetheart self, moving smoothly and evenly and flicking an ear back now and then as if to check to be sure she was doing exactly what her rider wanted.

Heather turned out to be a fast learner and it was easy to tell how much she liked it. Once when she was riding past she gave them one of her killer smiles and said, "I love it. I totally love it. I always knew I was going to—and I do."

Rudy couldn't help feeling sorry that she hadn't been able to learn to ride until now, just when she was about to go away to college. She'd go away and live in a city where she probably wouldn't have much chance to keep learning. But he felt good that he'd been the one to arrange for her to get the best kind of a start, at least.

Before very long Barney had her riding in figure eights, at a walk at first and then at a trot. Most of the time she remembered to keep her back straight and her heels down, and for a beginner she looked pretty good. Rudy and Barney both told her so.

"You're looking pretty good," Rudy yelled once. "Just keep easy-knees and your weight in your feet and you won't bounce so much."

Ty snorted and said, almost loud enough for Heather to hear, " 'Pretty good' doesn't touch it." Then he rolled his eyes and said, "Especially when she bounces."

"Shut up, Lewis," Barney said, and there was something about the way he said it that must have really gotten to Ty, because he didn't say anything more for quite a long time. When he did start talking again it wasn't about Heather. Instead he began to push for Barney to saddle up some of the other horses so that they could all ride.

Barney shook his head. "I don't know if you're ready for any of the other horses."

"Oh, yeah? Why not?" Ty said. "I'm not a green-horn anymore. You said yourself I was doing great. Rudy said so too." He leaned over and poked Rudy. "Didn't you, Chickie-baby?"

"Did I?" Rudy said.

Barney said, "Yeah, we said you were doing all right. But riding all right on Applesauce doesn't mean you're ready for the bucking bronc competition, you know." Then he leaned over and punched Ty's shoulder—making it look like a real knockout punch was coming, but pulling it at the last moment. "And I *told* you, Lewis, knock off that 'Chickie' business or I'm going to . . ." And he threw the pretend punch again.

"Sure, Barn," Ty said. "No more chicken business. Not even Kentucky Fried or McNuggets. But what's with this bucking bronc stuff? I'm not asking for any bucking bronc. What about that orange-colored dude old Rudy-baby was on yesterday?" Obviously Ty had been impressed by Badger's showy, head-tossing performance. "He didn't act like any bucking bronc. Just kind of lively, but that wouldn't bother me. What about me riding that one?"

"You mean Badger?" Barney said, grinning. "No, I don't think you're ready for old Badger yet."

"Oh, yeah?" Ty's eyes got their shiny plastic look. "Why not? Because you're saving him for old Ch . . . Rudy-baby." He looked at Rudy and curled his lip. "How about a little contest to see who gets the Badger horse, Drummond? How about a little arm wrestling or maybe a push-up contest? Best muscle gets the orange dude. Okay?"

It was about what Rudy expected. Ty was always trying to force him into some kind of physical strength contest. "To prove what?" he said, shrugging. "We already know you're the world's greatest hunk." Which wasn't the truth, of course. Barney was probably a lot stronger, although it hadn't been proven because Styler was careful never to challenge anyone his size. "Besides," Rudy went on, "horseback riding is one sport where sheer muscle power doesn't matter all that much. Right, Barney?''

Barney nodded and said "right" absentmindedly with his eyes on Heather and Applesauce. But later when Ty was still carrying on about wanting to ride Badger, and about how he knew he could do anything a little skinny dweeb like Rudy could do, Barney's eyes suddenly narrowed and he said, "All right, Styler. All right. You ride Badger. But don't say I didn't warn you."

Rudy was surprised. Barney knew better than to let people get in over their heads with horses. And it did look suspiciously like Barney had changed his mind just because he was ticked off at Ty about the "dweeb" remark. But using Badger to put Ty in his place was obviously not the world's greatest idea. Badger might pull one of his tricks and break Ty's neck or something.

On second thought, protecting old Styler's neck was not one of Rudy's major concerns—except that a broken neck was probably too much to hope for. What was more likely to happen was that Badger would totally freak Ty out and bring back his Shetland-Pony-from-Hell complex, which would mean the end of the whole riding school project.

A little later, when he and Barney were saddling the horses, Rudy brought the subject up. "About Styler and Badger," he said. "You sure you want to risk it? Hadn't you better ask your dad about it?"

"My dad and mom aren't home—as usual. They left this morning for Carson City. Granddad is, but he'd just say for me to do as I see fit. You know. That's what he usually says."

"Wouldn't it be better to put him on Bluebell, then?"

Barney just shrugged and grinned. "Let him try Badger," he said. "Maybe they'll get along great. You know, two of a kind."

"You mean two world-class show-offs?"

"Yeah, that. And cement-brained. Two cement-brained world-class show-offs. And anyway, Bluebell wouldn't be all that much safer. You know how spooky she is. If something wiggled the bushes, she'd be ten feet out from under him before he could catch his breath."

Barney was right. Bluebell was basically pretty gentle, but she was certainly spooky. She'd be going along nice and easy and then explode sideways at some sudden sound or motion. Once when he'd been riding her, helping Barney and his granddad round up some cattle, a pheasant flew up right in front of them. He wound up sitting in a thistle patch that day, and after that he never forgot to keep his weight in his feet and his eyes wide open when he was on Bluebell.

He quit arguing then and tried to stop worrying too. As he finished the saddling he told himself that if Ty was determined to get his stupid neck broken it would just have to happen and he, Rudy, might just as well relax and enjoy it.

All the time Rudy and Barney were getting the horses ready Ty had been over by the corral talking to Heather. Rudy couldn't hear what he was saying, but he was obviously putting on an "old cowhand" act, slapping Applesauce on the neck and rump, then checking out the cinch and stirrup straps like he was looking to see if anything was wrong with them. As if he would know if anything was. Or what to do about it.

As Rudy untied Bluebell and got on, he found himself wishing that Badger would really do a number on Styler—and then remembering why that wouldn't be a good idea and taking the wish back. He was still taking it back when Styler sauntered over to Badger and swung up into the saddle.

Badger didn't do anything unusual—just what he always did when a rider first got on. Which was to start tossing his head and dancing sideways, lifting his feet up high and snorting every few steps. The dancing bit wasn't anything dangerous if you knew how to handle it. You just had to use the reins and your heels to tell him gently but firmly that you had something else in mind and that he'd better forget about doing the samba and settle down to business. But of course what Ty did was exactly the wrong thing.

The minute Badger began to dance Ty started jerking back on the reins—hard. Real hard, as if he thought muscle power was going to make the difference. But this time he was up against a half ton of horseflesh, and sheer muscle power wasn't going to hack it. Not that Badger was necessarily trying to give him a bad time. It was just that he obviously thought all that jerking on the reins meant that he was supposed to back up, fast and hard. So he started going backward and the faster he went, the harder Ty pulled on the reins.

Barney yelled, "Ease up. Stop jerking the reins,"

but Ty kept shouting "Whoa" so loudly that he didn't hear, and Badger kept backing up. He went one way until he backed into the corral fence and then he whirled around and went the other way, still in reverse. And when Barney started running after them trying to grab the reins, he just reared up and went in a different direction.

Rudy would have tried to help, too, but he was already up on Bluebell when the commotion started, and of course the running and yelling and snorting spooked her out too. She shied sideways and tried to bolt and for a few seconds he had his hands too full to worry about what was happening to Styler. By the time Bluebell had settled down, Badger and Ty were clear across the barnyard and heading, still in reverse, straight for the thick hedge that separated the ranch house lawn from the rest of the yard. And when Badger's rump hit the prickly hedge he reared up—and dumped Styler right into the middle of it.

For a moment everything was quiet. Badger whirled around and froze, looking at Styler, or at what you could see of him. He'd landed on the flat top of the thick hedge in a sitting position, and kind of sunk in so that just his legs and head were sticking out. The big sorrel just stood there staring with his head cocked to one side like he was trying to figure out what kind of creature was in the hedge. But when Styler started to yell and kick he snorted and trotted away.

It wasn't easy getting Ty out. Barney had started trying right away and Rudy came to help as soon as he'd taken Bluebell and Badger back to the hitching rack. But the hedge was thick and prickly and when they tried pulling on the parts of Styler they could reach he kept swearing and yelling that they were killing him.

Heather was still up on Applesauce, but she rode over to watch, and when Ty yelled that he was dying, she put one hand up to her mouth and winced. Barney seemed worried, too, but Rudy kept having to struggle to keep from laughing. He felt a little guilty about it, but on the other hand, anybody who really was near death probably wouldn't be making that much noise. They'd finally managed to get Ty down by smashing a kind of channel down one side of the hedge, when Barney's grandfather came out of the house.

Charlie Crookshank came down the path moving slow and easy like always. He nodded at Rudy and touched his hat to Heather. Then he looked at the smashed-in hedge for quite a while and then down to where Ty was sitting on the ground examining his scratched-up arms and legs. Then he took off his beat-up old ten-gallon hat, dusted it with his sleeve, put it back on, and looked around again before he said, "You boys been up in the hedge?"

"No, Granddad," Barney said. "Not Rudy and me. Just Ty here."

Charlie nodded for quite a while. "Why's that?" he said finally.

"Badger threw him up there," Barney said.

Charlie nodded some more before he grinned and said, "Looks like he needs a little patching up. Bring him on into the house." He turned and headed back down the path. Halfway there he stopped and said to Heather, "You come in, too, young lady."

Inside the big modern but rustic-looking kitchen, Rudy and Barney and Heather stood around watching while Charlie got out his first-aid kit and doctored Ty's scratches and punctures. He had quite a lot of them on his arms and face, and a few on his legs where some twigs had poked through the stylish holes in his jeans. The medicine in Charlie's kit was just plain old iodine instead of some modern "ouchless" stuff, and Ty did a lot of complaining about it. But by the time the doctoring was finished he was more or less back to normal, enjoying being the center of attention and wising off about how he'd always known that all horses were demons sent from hell especially to get Tyler J. Lewis III. And how he wasn't going to forget it again. Then he insisted on calling his dad's office to get a ride home.

"Your dad doesn't have to come way out here," Heather told him. "You can ride home with Rudy and me as soon as I'm finished with my lesson." She looked hopefully at Barney. "I'm not quite finished yet, am I?"

"Finished?" Barney said quickly. "No. Not finished."

Heather said, "Oh, good," and gave him one of her killer smiles. But Ty said he didn't want to wait so he called his father, and pretty soon the Mercedes roared into the ranch yard and Ty limped out and got in. And when old Styler had disappeared over the far horizon Rudy and Barney and Heather went for a short ride in the hills.

They only went as far as the gate to the east pasture, but on the way Barney loosened up and the three of them had a good time talking about horses and riding. And there were a few mentions of Tyler Lewis, of course. Every time someone mentioned his name all three cracked up.

"I can't help it," Heather said, and then giggled again before she could go on. "I just keep seeing his head and legs sticking out of that hedge."

"Yeah," Barney said. "And old Badger standing there looking at him—like he couldn't figure out what he was doing up there."

That gave Rudy an idea. "Hey," he said. "You know what? I think old Styler may have invented a new gymnastic sport called 'hedge vaulting.' "

"Yeah," Barney said. "One of those long-horse stunts. You vault off the horse and land in the hedge." Mr. Jacobs, the P.E. teacher at Pyramid Hill Middle School, was into gymnastics, so they all knew about things like long horses and parallel bars and balance beams.

"You got it," Rudy said. "Off a long horse—preferably a sorrel but any good long horse will do—and right into the hedge."

They laughed so hard they almost spooked Bluebell, and when they finally calmed down Heather said in a very serious tone of voice, "And you get the most points for a really good dismount and landing," and they all fell apart all over again. By the time they got back to the barnyard Rudy's stomach ached from laughing.

Chapter 9

RUDY WOKE UP the next morning feeling pretty good. On the one hand, the riding school project was probably finished, at least as far as Ty was concerned, but the good news was that maybe it didn't matter anymore. Maybe Barney had finally seen through the old Ty-wanese Kid and had enough of him. And without Ty around to egg him on, Rudy was pretty sure he could talk Barney out of the whole gold-mining scheme. Particularly now that there was Heather and the riding lessons to occupy his mind.

But that same evening—it was Wednesday and Rudy had survived another long afternoon of baby-sitting—he found out differently. Natasha and the M and M's had gone downtown right after dinner and Rudy was alone in the house, except for Ophelia. After reading the funnies and checking the TV schedule, he decided to call Barney. The conversation had started off about the riding lesson and Heather, but then the subject of Tyler Lewis came up, and it seemed that Barney had been talking to him on the phone.

"You called Styler up?" Rudy asked, and bit his tongue to keep from asking why.

"Yeah," Barney said. "Just to see how he was getting along. Like, if he had blood poisoning or tetanus or anything. He could have, you know, with all those punctures. Punctures are how you get tetanus."

"Yeah, so I've heard," Rudy said. "Well, did he? Have tetanus?"

"Guess not. He didn't even want to talk about it. All he wanted to talk about was how he'd figured out a way to solve the lamp problem. You know. The one on his miner's helmet."

"You mean that carbide thing," Rudy asked. "I did a report on those things once. They were pretty dangerous. They make this flammable gas when water drips into the carbide stuff and then there's a switch that hits a flint that makes a spark. Then if you're lucky you get a flame. And if you're unlucky you get a minor explosion, and maybe burn off your eyebrows."

Barney laughed. "Yeah, that's what Ty found out. He said he singed himself a few times, so he went another route. He kind of smashed the lamp part down and taped a flashlight on top of the helmet instead. He said I ought to fix mine the same way."

Rudy felt something heavy hit the bottom of his stomach with a thud. "Yours?" he asked in what he hoped wasn't a quavery voice. "You mean, you have one too?"

"No," Barney said. "Not yet."

Not just "no." That wouldn't have been so bad, although something like, "No, and I don't want one," would have been even better. But "not yet"? That could only mean one thing.

The conversation fizzled out after that, and as soon as Rudy hung up the phone he kind of lurched across the room and dropped into a chair at the kitchen table.

So, the gold-mining scheme was still in the works. He couldn't believe it. What he found hardest to believe, in fact, was that Barney could still be interested in doing anything at all with Tyler Lewis, now that he'd been shown up as a cement-brained, loud-mouthed show-off. *And a chicken besides.*

A chicken. Tyler Lewis was a chicken. A strange raging tornado was building up inside Rudy's head. He crashed his fist down on the table and then jumped up and kicked the chair he'd been sitting in so hard that it tipped over. Across the room Ophelia leaped to her feet and began to bark.

"Shut up, you nerdy dog," Rudy yelled, and stormed out of the kitchen and down the hall. In his own room he collapsed sideways across his bed and covered his face with his arm.

With Natasha and the girls away it was very quiet in the house. No sound at all at first and then only an occasional whimper from Ophelia, who had followed him into the room and was now snuffling nervously at his feet.

"Shut up, Ophelia," he said again, but this time with a lot less energy. The raging anger was getting away from him, no matter how hard he tried to hang on to it. And the thing was, he knew that when it was gone he was going to start thinking, and that was exactly what he didn't want to do.

He was going to have to start thinking about why that word "chicken" had made him so angry. It had, all right. He'd started losing it the minute he'd thought of calling Ty a chicken—and the reason, of course, was that getting angry took the place of admitting the truth. The truth! Which was, of course, that it wasn't Ty Lewis who was the real major-league, world-class chicken. But that was exactly what he definitely *wasn't going to think about.*

And he wasn't going to waste time making up excuses for himself either. Useless excuses about not wanting to do something that was not only dangerous but also against the law, which did *not* mean you were chicken—it only meant you were sensible. Useless because he knew—knew absolutely—that the reason he couldn't and wouldn't and never would—no matter what—go down into that hole in the ground was because the very thought of it *scared him to death.* And that had to mean something.

Rudy jumped to his feet, started across the room, tripped over Ophelia, crashed into the dresser, hopped around holding his right knee and his left elbow while saying a few unprintable things under his breath, and then managed to make it out the door. He stormed down the hall, through the kitchen and the studio, into the living room, and out the front door. Standing on the veranda he looked down Lone Pine toward town, but there was no sign of Natasha and the M and M's. Wasn't that just like women. Always underfoot when you didn't want them to be and never there when you needed them. Like when you really needed somebody —anybody—to talk to.

It was strangely quiet on the veranda too. The weird silence that he'd noticed in the house seemed to be everywhere. No noisy tourists around and not even any traffic sounds drifting up from downtown. Nothing except for a faint, familiar sound—the clickety-clack of a typewriter. Murph.

Murph came to the door looking even more rumpled than usual. His corkscrew hair was standing out all around his head and he was wearing a ratty old bathrobe over his usual jeans and long-sleeved undershirt. For a moment his eyes looked blank and unfocused, as if he were having trouble relating to what his eyes were seeing. As if his mind was still busy with whatever it was he'd been writing. But then he got back to normal.

"Rudy," he said, smiling warmly. "Come on in."

Rudy felt guilty. Although he'd always been in the habit of visiting Murph pretty much whenever he felt like it, he'd never done it before when the typewriter was going. He'd always kind of felt that, since Murph was a writer who very rarely got it together to do any writing, it didn't seem right to interrupt him when he did.

"I—I guess you're busy," Rudy said, starting to back away.

"Well . . ." Murph began, and then stopped and

gave Rudy his narrow-eyed "student of humanity" stare. "No," he said. "Not very busy. Come right on in, my boy. I was just about to knock off anyway and have a bit of refreshment. How about joining me in a cup of coffee?"

Rudy thought of saying that he didn't think they'd fit—but then decided against it. Somehow he just didn't have the energy to wise off even when such a cheap shot presented itself. Instead he just nodded, gulped at the lump in his throat, managed a squeaky, "Thanks," and followed Murph into the kitchen.

By the time they were both seated at the table with cups of coffee—with a lot of milk and sugar in Rudy's case, since Murph's coffee was always industrial strength—his voice, at least, had gotten back to normal. But what he started talking about, of course, had nothing to do with what had made him desperate enough to interrupt the writing of the great Murph Woodbury novel. What he started talking about was Heather and the riding lesson.

Of course, Murph knew all about the inheritance. That was the kind of information that any "student of humanity" worth his salt would be right on top of. He'd also heard, it so happened, a bit about the lesson at Lawford's.

"I stopped by the Hanrahans on Sunday morning and heard all about it," he said. "It seems the riding-stables lesson was a qualified success."

"Right," Rudy said. "It was pretty much of a wipeout, I guess. So I fixed it up for her to get some lessons from Barney. On Applesauce. You know, Angela's barrel racing horse."

96

"Ah, yes," Murph said. "The pretty dapple-gray mare. I've seen Angela riding the gray in the barrel race event at the Penn Valley Rodeo. Beautiful animal. And how did the lesson go?"

So Rudy told him all about it, including Ty's part. How Ty had his first riding lesson on Monday, and decided that he was the world's greatest natural-born horseman. And how yesterday, he'd insisted on riding Badger and had wound up sitting in the hedge.

He really enjoyed telling Murph about that, and about the ride afterward and what a good time he and Barney and Heather had, and how they'd made up all the stuff about the new gymnastic event called hedge vaulting. By the time he'd finished, Murph was laughing and so was Rudy—and feeling a lot better.

Then Murph stopped laughing and said, "So. What do you suppose Barney sees in this Ty character?"

Rudy looked up quickly. As usual, Murph had picked up on the really heavy stuff without its even being mentioned. At least not in so many words.

Rudy shrugged. "Who knows? I guess they have some things in common. I guess they both like to . . . well, kind of live dangerously. You know, do stuff like . . ." But he couldn't get into that. "Hey," he said instead. "I'm sorry I interrupted your writing. What are you working on these days, anyway? You've really been going at it lately. I heard your typewriter this morning and then again tonight."

Murph grinned. "Yes, you're right. I have been a bit more fired up than usual. The other day I got out an old novel I started years ago and when I read it over it sounded—well, better than I remembered. So . . ."

"Oh, yeah? What's it about?"

"About a young woman. A gifted, spirited young woman who had a particular problem that pretty much ruined her life. Actually the central character is loosely based on my mother. Perhaps you've heard something about my mother?"

Rudy nodded, trying not to look embarrassed. What he'd heard was that Murph's mother had been crazy. Of course, she'd been dead for years and years, but in a town like Pyramid Hill where a lot of families had been around for generations, rumors like that hung around for a long time.

Murph was waiting for an answer. "Well, yes. I guess what I heard was . . ."

"That she was insane? Well, that isn't true, you know. My mother was quite normal except in one limited but very significant way. It was just that she suffered from a particular phobia. Do you know about phobias, Rudy?"

Rudy thought he did. "Isn't it when you're really afraid of something? Like, they used to call rabies 'hydrophobia' because they thought anyone who had it was afraid of water."

"Right," Murph said. "But the word implies something more than just being afraid. What it implies is a terrible unreasoned panic in someone who is, otherwise, quite normal. In my mother's case it was obviously agoraphobia, although it was never formally diagnosed."

"Agoraphobia?" Rudy asked.

"Yes. Literally, fear of the marketplace. But what it means to a victim is a growing fear of any sort of open space. Until they are finally confined to their own home, or even to a single room. My poor mother went from being a happy and normal young mother to being less and less able to go anywhere. For the last twenty years of her life she never set foot outside the walls of this dark old house. And yet she was quite normal in other ways."

After that Murph really got wound up, like he did sometimes, when he started telling about things that happened a long time ago. He went on and on about his mother's problem and how she had to give up going to church and to friends' houses and even to the store, and how people gradually got to think of her as a kind of mental case, and finally no one even came to see her.

It was an interesting story in a depressing sort of way, but right at first Rudy was only mildly curious. It all seemed, like a lot of Murph's stories, out of date and not related to modern everyday life. It wasn't until Murph started in on what happened when his mother tried to "pull herself together" like everyone kept telling her to do, and "force herself to go right on outside," that Rudy really began to listen carefully.

"A terrible blind panic," Murph called it. "Racing heart, shortness of breath, and uncontrollable feelings of terror . . ." And somewhere in the midst of Murph's story something suddenly went off in Rudy's head. Like an explosion going off.

"A blind panic about certain ordinary things," Murph had said. Things like crawling under a house or

getting locked in a storage cupboard. *"A crazy blind panic in someone who was quite normal in other ways."* Quite normal—like someone who was maybe a natural-born extrovert and probably the second most popular guy at Pyramid Hill Middle School. *"A racing heart, shortness of breath, and uncontrollable feelings of terror . . ."* The words kept repeating themselves in his head.

After that his mind was so busy with other things, he wasn't really listening to Murph anymore and it must have been quite a while later that he realized that it was quiet in the kitchen. Murph had quit talking and was just doing the narrow-eyed bit in Rudy's general direction.

Rudy got to his feet, thanked Murph for the coffee, and headed out the door. He was partway down the back steps when he turned around and ran back.

"Murph," he said as he threw the kitchen door open. "About these phobia things. Isn't there anything you can do about them? I mean are they like, incurable, or what?"

Murph came out onto the back porch. He stared at Rudy for several seconds before he said, "Very little was ever done to help the victims of phobias when I was young. But I've read that nowadays there are several methods of therapy that have been used successfully for treating people who suffer from various kinds of phobias. Just the other day I read—"

But at that moment Natasha came out on the veranda and shouted for Rudy to come home.

"I couldn't imagine where you were," she called.

"Come along home now and stop bothering poor Murph."

Murph gave Rudy his sneaky "we're in this together" grin. "Another time," he said. "We'll talk some more another time."

So Rudy went home and looked at the stuff Natasha and the M and M's had bought and listened to a quarrel about who was going to get the pink tutu and who was going to get stuck with the other one. It was after nine o'clock before he was able to get away to his own room and think—about phobias.

Chapter 10

THERE WASN'T A WHOLE LOT about phobias in the encyclopedia in the children's room of the library, but there were a few interesting bits of information—like a list of the most common ones. Rudy had heard about some of them before, without knowing their scientific names. He knew about acrophobia, for instance, in which people were so afraid of high places that they couldn't go up in airplanes or even in tall buildings, but he hadn't known what it was called scientifically.

There were others, however, that he'd never heard of at all, like gatophobia (fear of cats). That struck him as a little bit weird. He got one of his vivid mental pictures—a big muscle-bound guy cringing in a corner, trying to hide from a fluffy little blob of a kitten. But then, a phobia was a phobia, and he supposed gatophobia made as much sense as any. There wasn't any mention of fear of dogs, or cows, but he supposed some people had hang-ups about them too. Not to mention horses. He snickered. Like Shetland Ponies from Hell. Maybe he'd make up a name for Ty's phobia and tell Barney and Heather about it. Pintophobia, maybe?

Another one he didn't recognize right off was nyctophobia. Who'd ever heard of nyctophobia? Probably not one percent of the millions of people who'd probably had it. Like most little kids who'd ever lived—including Rudolph W. Drummond. Nyctophobia, it turned out, meant fear of the dark.

Rudy chuckled out loud this time and Mrs. Carnaby, the librarian, looked over at him questioningly. When he shrugged and grinned at her she went on looking curious for a second or two before she smiled and went back to sorting some cards. Mrs. Carnaby was used to Rudy—he'd been one of her most constant customers ever since he'd learned to read. She'd helped him on lots of research projects, including the famous bastards thing, and the one comparing court jesters to modern comedians. She was also used to the fact that he laughed at a lot of stuff that wouldn't strike most people as particularly hilarious—like the encyclopedia.

Under other circumstances he probably would have taken time to explain what he was laughing about, but he was in a hurry and besides, he wasn't sure if Mrs. Carnaby would get much of a kick out of hearing about how, when he was a little kid, probably four or five years old, he used to break all existing speed records on his way down the dark hall to the bathroom. Natasha had scolded him a hundred times for always waiting until it was an emergency, but as far as he could remember, he never did set her straight. He never clued her in to the fact that the danger was not that he might wet his pants. The danger was, of course, that he would be eaten alive if he gave the Monsters of the Dark time to get their act together before he made it to the light switch.

So there apparently were temporary phobias, like the ones people tended to outgrow—the encyclopedia called them "mild" phobias. And then there were others. Like agoraphobia (fear of open spaces), which was what had ruined Murph's mother's life. And then there was claustrophobia.

Claustrophobia. That was what he'd been looking for, but except for saying that it meant the fear of confined spaces, the encyclopedia didn't have much to offer. He'd heard of claustrophobia, of course. He'd always thought of it in terms of people who didn't like being in small rooms or in anything but aisle seats on airplanes and in theaters, but he hadn't ever related it to himself. After all, his bedroom was pretty small and that had never bothered him, and he'd never had any problem with elevators or middle-of-the-row seats. It wasn't until last night's conversation with Murph that he'd thought of his problem as maybe relating to claustrophobia.

Besides the list of scientific names and what they meant, the article in the encyclopedia included a short general paragraph that said a phobia was an intense fear focused on a specific circumstance or idea, and that it was a fear that tended to be "excessive, inappropriate, and without obvious cause." Right! Like having a world-class case of the screaming meemies when your little sister locks you in a closet.

As Rudy put away the encyclopedia he realized that he was feeling encouraged. So there was a name for it, and even a reason. A reason other than just general chickenhood, that is. Of course, he knew that just having a name for something didn't mean you had it licked. At some point Mrs. Woodbury might have found out that what she had was agoraphobia, but that probably wouldn't have cured her of it. But Murph had started to say something about some new therapies that helped people with phobias.

He thought of asking Mrs. Carnaby where he might find some more information, and then decided against it. Instead he just told her good-bye, put away the encyclopedia, and went down to the adult department. It was there in the card catalogue that he found just what he was looking for. A whole book on the subject called *Conquering Your Fears* by Dr. Melvin Grosser. It was a thick book and judging by the first page it didn't seem like it was going to be particularly easy reading. Not easy, but possibly *very* enlightening. Some of the chapters listed in the contents had titles like Traditional Therapeutic Approaches and Recent Experimental Treatment Techniques. Rudy checked the book out and took it home.

The next morning, after he'd gotten the M and M's off to Eleanora's he started reading, but he'd barely gotten into it when Mr. Williard, a neighbor on Lone Pine, called up and asked if he'd like a lawn mowing job that morning. Since, at the moment, he happened to be even more broke than usual, he decided he'd better do it. The Williards' lawn wasn't big, but it was complicated by all sorts of little flower beds and rock gardens, and by the time it was finished the morning was almost over.

Then the M and M's got home and he gave up on *Conquering Your Fears* at least for the time being. He knew the two of them too well to clue them in on phobias. He could just imagine what Moira, in particular, could do with that kind of information. Like coming down with a bad case of dustaphobia (fear of cleaning up your room) or vegaphobia (fear of eating your carrots and peas). So the reading material for the afternoon turned out to be "Cinderella" and "Lady and the Tramp." Talk about Yawn City.

He'd probably read "Cinderella" to the M and M's several hundred times, but this time it turned out to be a little more entertaining. Somehow, maybe because he was in a hopeful frame of mind, he started putting a little more into it, and he wound up acting out some of the parts. He set up a stage in the bay window, and made little costumes with pillows and doilies and scarfs when he was being the evil stepsisters. The part the M and M's particularly liked was when he emerged from behind the drapes as the fairy godmother wearing one of Natasha's tutus and waving a plumber's friend for a magic wand.

Later when he was in the kitchen getting the cookies and milk ready he overheard Moira saying, "Rudy is the best story reader in the whole world." And the amazing part was that Margot agreed with her, which was probably one of the few things they'd agreed on since they'd learned to talk.

After dinner that night he tried to get into the phobia book again, but he'd no more than gotten settled in the living room when Natasha came in. Rudy shoved the book under the couch pillow.

He didn't know why, exactly, except that he wasn't ready to talk to her about the phobia thing. As far as he knew, Natasha didn't even know about his screaming meemies problem. She hadn't been around when the worst attacks had happened, except for the time Moira had locked him in the storage closet. And even then she'd only gotten home in time to get in on the end of it, and she'd apparently thought it was just an extradramatic temper tantrum. And he'd never even tried to tell her what it had really been like. He didn't know why exactly, except that Natasha had to depend on him for a lot of things since old Art bailed out, and she'd had a hard enough time without having to worry that he was about to crack up and fink out on her too.

So the book stayed under the pillow and Natasha settled down on the other end of the couch. She'd finished getting the M and M's to bed and seemed to be in a talkative mood.

At first she told him about her day at work and then they got into the subject of the riding lessons and Heather Hanrahan and Heather's inheritance.

"I think it's so great," Natasha said. "No one could deserve it more. I just hope that great uncle of hers is getting all sorts of brownie points in heaven for leaving that money to Heather. You know, the Hanrahans were totally surprised when they found out about it.

Heather came over to tell me about it the day she found out and she was so thrilled and excited. It's great that she's going to be able to go away to college. Of course, we're all going to miss her around here."

"Tell me about it," Rudy said. "All the professional girl watchers in Pyramid Hill are going to go into mourning. Not to mention a lot of other people. Everyone's going to miss her."

Natasha was certainly one of the people who would miss Heather. They'd been good friends ever since Rudy was just a little kid and Heather used to take him and some other little kids in the neighborhood over to her house to play school. She was a good teacher, too, even when she was only a kid herself. Natasha always said it was probably because of the good start Rudy had gotten with Heather that he'd always been at the top of his class in reading.

"You're right," Natasha said. "Everyone's crazy about Heather."

"Right!" Rudy said. "And you know who especially? Barney Crookshank. Barney really has it bad for Heather. I mean, it seems kind of pointless. A guy like Barney who has every girl his age in the whole town drooling over him, and he never even notices. And then he goes into a major seizure over someone who's terminally unavailable. Like four years older, for one thing."

"Really," Natasha said. "Is it that serious?" And then she sighed and added, "Poor little Barney."

Rudy snorted. "Poor?" he said. "What's poor about Barney? Or little, for that matter?" He could think of a lot of adjectives to describe Barney Crookshank, but "poor" had certainly never been one of them.

"Well . . ." Natasha said. Then she shook her head and looked away, as if she'd decided against what she'd been about to say.

"Poor?" Rudy insisted.

"Everybody has problems," Natasha said. "Even Barney."

"Sure," Rudy said. "Big problems. Like being great-looking and a world-class athlete—and having parents who are practically famous and have lots of money, and who let you do anything you want. And living in a great place like the Crooked Bar Ranch. Sure wish I had some of Barney's problems."

He'd not meant to sound bitter or jealous or anything, but maybe he did, because when he finally ran down Natasha was staring at him in a funny way as if what he'd said had made her angry or maybe just depressed. Then she sighed and picked up the paper and started to read, and when Rudy said "Mom?" she just said "shh" with her finger to her lips.

"Shh, Rudy. No more about problems tonight, please. I'm just too tired."

And since having a serious phobia in the family would probably be considered in the problem category, the book by Dr. Grosser stayed right where it was, under the couch pillow.

It wasn't until Rudy was in bed that night that he was able to get back into phobia research. After skimming over the chapter headings he picked out the section about recent experimental treatments as being the most interesting and started reading there.

Some of it was so full of technical and scientific language that it didn't make a whole lot of sense, but there was one part that seemed like it might be useful. It was about some psychologists who had worked out a method of treatment called "implosion." What they did was to get their patients to imagine the worst. Like a lady who was so afraid of spiders that she couldn't go anywhere or do anything for fear she might meet one was treated by having her imagine over and over again that spiders were everywhere, even all over her clothes and hands and face. The treatment really freaked her out at first, but after a while she began to get over it and finally she wasn't overly afraid of spiders at all anymore.

Okay, he thought. The implosion method. According to Dr. Grosser all you had to do was "Picture as realistically as possible whatever it is you are most afraid of." It sounded simple enough. All you had to do was imagine—something that Rudy had always been good at. He closed his eyes and lay back on the pillows.

Imagine . . . darkness and enclosing walls. The darkness came quickly, reaching out around him. And then the walls were there, shutting him in. The dark was hard and heavy and it covered his face and stopped his breathing. Crushing, smothering, endless darkness that . . .

He was out of bed then, without even knowing how he'd gotten there. Out of bed and pacing up and down, up and down, willing his heart to stop racing, and fighting to keep down the sound that ached in his throat. Seven steps to the dresser and seven back to the bed. Count the steps. One, two, three, four . . . Don't think about anything else. Only the counting and walking and breathing. Deep breathing, deep, deep breaths of good, clean air.

After what seemed like a very long time his heart-beat slowed and his breathing began to be easier, and by the time he climbed back into bed he was pretty much back to normal except for slightly shaky hands and an occasional shudder or two.

Okay, Rudy, old buddy, he told himself. So much for the implosion method.

Chapter 11

WHEN RUDY GOT BACK into bed after the implosion disaster the first thing he did was throw the book by Dr. Grosser across the room. Then he turned out the light and pulled the covers up to his chin, keeping his eyes wide open. If he kept his mind firmly on what he could really see he wouldn't be able to picture anything "as realistically as possible." Particularly not "whatever it is you are most afraid of."

He could see the foot of the bed quite clearly in the bright moonlight, and beyond it the old oak dresser that, according to Natasha, had been in the same spot even way back when she was a little girl and the room had been hers. He stared at the dresser, concentrating on the details of the old-fashioned golden oak mirror frame and trying to make out all the photos and souvenirs that he'd stuck in under the edge. When that got boring he switched to trying to picture how it might have looked when it was Natasha's—covered with girl stuff and with maybe a tutu hanging from one of the mirror's support poles.

Yes, a tutu for sure. Natasha, or Linda as she had been called then, had told him that she'd known she wanted to be a ballet dancer when she was only four or five years old, just as he had always known he wanted to be an actor and comedian. When he concentrated he could almost see her, a little girl with long, fat pigtails, spinning around the room in a tutu.

It was something he hadn't really thought much about before—Natasha as a kid planning her future. And now, thinking about how her life had turned out made him feel a little angry at fate, or maybe at people. People like old Art Mumford, and his own father for that matter. Or whoever's fault it was that Natasha didn't get to make her dream come true. He thought about it for quite a while and the good news was that feeling angry for Natasha turned out to be a great way to keep his mind off other things. He went on working at feeling angry about the way fate had treated Natasha until he fell asleep.

It wasn't until midmorning the next day that Rudy managed to talk himself into fishing the phobia book out from under his desk. After all, he told himself as he kicked back on the bed in a comfortable reading position, he hadn't finished reading about all the other methods of treating phobia patients. There was no reason to give up just because the *implosion* method had been such a complete wipeout.

The next method of treatment that Dr. Grosser went into was something that he called "progressive challenges." The idea seemed to be that the patients were to take small gradual steps toward conquering their fear. It gave as an example the case of a woman who had agoraphobia—the same problem that Murph's mother had. At first the patient was asked to stand in the open doorway of her home. Only for a minute or two at first, but gradually increasing the time. Then she sat in a chair on the veranda, and next out on the lawn. She was supposed to concentrate on pushing herself to go a little longer and a little farther, but at the same time reminding herself that she was free to go back inside any time she felt she had to.

Rudy liked that part. The being free to back out at any time. It seemed like a person could stand almost anything if he felt sure he could stop it anytime he wanted to. But on further consideration it occurred to him that there was a major difference in the two situations. In the case of the woman with agoraphobia, what she was gradually moving toward was something pleasant, like going downtown and shopping and meeting people. And in his case what he would be moving toward would be doing something not only terrifying but also dangerous and illegal—going down into an abandoned mine. Down into a dark, airless . . .

No! He was getting ahead of himself. The point was that you had to move slowly and gradually. Gradually. That was the key word. But in the meantime he went on to read about a third method of treatment that turned out to be something called "attitude readjustment."

Attitude readjustment, it seemed, was changing how you felt about whatever you were afraid of by having things you particularly like happen to you when you were in the scary situation. Like the woman with agoraphobia was treated especially nice by her family and served things she particularly liked to eat while she was sitting outside the house. And a girl who had acrophobia so bad that she couldn't even go near a window in a tall building, had her boyfriend go with her as she went up in a skyscraper. Then the boyfriend was supposed to do what the book called "offer expressions of affection" whenever they were near stairwells or open windows.

Now, that was a treatment Rudy could definitely relate to. He could really see how it might work for him, especially if someone like Stephanie Freeman would do the "expressions of affection" bit. Realistically, however, he had to admit that he'd probably never get Stephanie to make out with him in an abandoned gold mine. Stephanie just wasn't the type to fool around in a place like that. Particularly not with someone she'd already turned down in perfectly normal places, like out behind the multipurpose room during school dances.

But, on second thought, there was the storage closet. There was just a chance that she might agree to the closet, if he could come up with the right approach. Maybe if he made it into a kind of scientific experiment. Stephanie was really into science, entering exhibits in all the science fairs and that sort of thing. What he could do was explain the claustrophobia problem and the "attitude readjustment" thing and ask her if she'd like to be part of a scientific experiment to see how well the treatment worked. She might really go for that kind of an approach, especially if he could think of some way to make it into a science fair exhibit.

It was, he decided, worth a try. But in the meantime it might be a good idea for him to practice a little, just to be sure he could pull it off, without completely freaking out. It would be all right if he were a little nervous about crawling into the closet with Stephanie. Perfect, in fact. She'd expect that. But a serious case of the screaming meemies would probably be more than she would bargain for. So he'd just have to do a preliminary experiment or two. Marking his place in *Conquering Your Fears,* he hid it under the mattress before he left the room.

In the front hall Rudy stood for a moment breathing deeply and trying to center his mind on Stephanie before he pulled back the latch on the closet door, swung it open, and peered in. The storage closet, situated as it was under the stairs, was really more of a cupboard than a real closet. It was only about four feet tall at the highest point and from there it tapered back to nothing at the small end.

The light was dim, but as his eyes adjusted he was able to make out a bunch of winter boots in one corner, the M and M's roller skates in another, and a stack of boxes and foot lockers against the back wall. It all looked very familiar, which wasn't surprising, since in the past he'd used the closet a lot. For years he'd kept his skateboard and baseball stuff there, and before that when he was a real little kid he'd even used it as a place to play. He could vaguely remember some game about a dragon's lair.

And that, now that he thought about it, was pretty strange—that when he was really little he'd crawled around in the closet, and curled up way down at the small end, and it hadn't bothered him at all. And right up until last year he'd been able to keep his stuff there without any problems. But then, ever since last Christmas when Moira locked him in, he had not so much as opened the door until now.

There was no light switch in the closet, and no window. Fighting back an urge to slam the door and walk away, Rudy reminded himself of what he was intending to do—to sit in the closet and imagine making out with Stephanie. He was going to crawl way back beyond the boxes and . . . but gradually. It was important not to forget about gradually. Sitting down in the hallway, he put his feet inside the closet up to his ankles, closed his eyes, and began to imagine. Once or twice he opened his eyes and scooted an inch or so forward, but half an hour later when the M and M's pounded up onto the front veranda, he hadn't gotten very far. At least he hadn't gotten very far into the closet. He'd made all sorts of progress with Stephanie. Too bad it was all in his imagination.

As it turned out, that was the last phobia treatment Rudy tried for several days—not that he'd given up on the whole experiment. Even though his lack of progress had been a disappointment, he really did intend to go on trying. It was just that he seemed to be extra busy for a while.

For one thing, he was spending a lot of time at Murph's helping him learn to use his new word processor. There had been a computer club at school and Rudy had found out that he was just naturally computer friendly. So when Murph finally got a word processor—he'd been talking about it for years—Rudy was able to help him out. The problem seemed to be that Murph hated his computer. At least he did at first.

"It never does what I want it to," he told Rudy over the back fence. "I give it a perfectly reasonable command and it just says 'invalid entry' and then sits there smirking at me. I came dangerously close to using an ax on it several times yesterday."

So Rudy went over to see if he could help. The computer was another Apple, like the ones at school, but a newer model. It wasn't all that different, however, and that first morning it didn't take Rudy very long to find out what Murph had been doing wrong. But for the next few days other problems kept coming up, so Rudy kept having to go back, reread the instruction books, and try things out until he came up with another solution.

In between word processor discussions, Rudy and Murph managed to get in quite a bit of general conversation on other topics as well—like the whole phobia thing. Without mentioning why he had any particular reason to be interested, Rudy simply told Murph that his story about his mother's agoraphobia had gotten him interested and he'd started a research project on the general subject.

"I was really surprised how many different kinds of phobias there are," he told Murph. "A person can hit the panic button about just about anything, I guess. Cats, rats, spiders, snakes, germs, high places, escalators, doctors, people in uniforms. I mean, you name it, there's somebody who's scared to death of it. In fact, I'm thinking of working up a stand-up comedian routine about people with phobias. You know, like one about a guy who has this deathly fear of anchovy pizzas, or something."

Murphy, who was straightening things up and putting his computer's dustcover on for the night, chuckled and said he guessed phobias were extremely numerous all right, not to mention very common. "Almost all of us probably have one or two, or have had at some point in our lives. Fortunately most of them are fairly mild or quite temporary."

"Right," Rudy said, "like nyctophobia, for instance. Probably ninety-nine kids out of a hundred are afraid of the dark when they're little." Then he told Murph about how he used to dash down the hall on his way to the bathroom. "I'd go . . ." he said, and started acting it out—the bulgy-eyed peek down the dark hall, the frantic dash, and then, once he'd made it to the light switch, the smug look back over his shoulder at all the frustrated monsters.

Murph was still chuckling when Rudy checked his watch and made another frantic dash—this time for home. The M and M's were due back from Eleanora's.

The other thing that was taking up a lot of Rudy's time was, of course, the baby-sitting, which was turning out to be a little less boring than he expected it would be. He couldn't say why exactly, but it probably had something to do with his natural instinct to find out about things. What he'd started researching this time was the M and M's themselves, like trying to find out why they fought so much, for instance.

A lot of the problem seemed to be because of the differences in their personalities. Of course, he'd always been aware that even though Moira and Margot were sisters and only about a year apart in age, they weren't really much alike, but he'd never given the subject much thought. Researching Moira and Margot, which involved a lot of observation, interrogation, and even some visits to the library, turned out to be very enlightening.

The observation was easy. Moira and Margot were so used to having Rudy around that they usually went on doing whatever came naturally, whether he was watching or not. Even when he came right into their room while they were playing.

The room itself was pretty interesting when observed scientifically. Of course, he'd noticed before that one half of the M and M's room looked more lived in than the other, but he'd never been interested enough to figure out why. But as soon as he started doing a careful examination it quickly became obvious what was going on. Everything had been divided so that Margot's belongings were on one side of the room and all of Moira's stuff was on the other. And while Margot's half was fairly neat and well organized, Moira's usually looked like the scene of some kind of minor explosion. The only thing they couldn't divide was Blob, their fat little pet hamster, so his cage sat right in the middle of the room—and even Moira's half of the hamster cage looked a lot less sanitary. Rudy felt that was a particularly significant bit of research data.

The library visit wasn't, strictly speaking, a research trip. There weren't any reference books, at least none that Rudy could find, about seven- and eight-year-old sisters who'd been trying to dogmeat each other since they were in diapers. The visits to the library had simply been to help them pick out some books to borrow, since Rudy was pretty sick of the ones they'd had before. But the trip proved interesting anyway when he considered what books they picked out—and why.

Moira liked all sorts of weird stuff like fairy tales and ghost stories and mysteries, and the longer the book, the better; while Margot liked short books with lots of pictures of scientific things like animals and bugs.

As for the interrogation part of the M and M research, all that involved was talking to them, sometimes together, but more importantly, when they were separate. The talking was the most enlightening part of the whole research project, which kind of surprised Rudy until he realized that he'd never really talked to his sisters all that much before. He'd entertained them some, and yelled at them a lot—but there hadn't been all that much talking.

Rudy had a particularly interesting discussion with Moira one evening when he happened to find her alone in the living room. Natasha and Margot were in the kitchen at the time baking cookies and singing

"I've Been Working on the Railroad." Natasha always sang while she cooked because she hated cooking and singing took her mind off it. Margot, on the other hand, loved cooking. Especially baking cookies. Margot said that making cookies was her second favorite hobby, right after her first favorite—eating cookies.

"Where's Moira?" Rudy had to shout to be heard over a noisy chorus of *"someone's in the kitchen with Dinah."* Natasha pointed toward the living room.

Moira was curled up in the ratty old overstuffed chair that used to be Art's. Her sleek dark head was bent over a book. Moira read a lot for an eight-year-old.

"Hi," Rudy said. "What are you reading?"

She held up the book. "This. *The Little Princess.* Margot said it would be too hard for me. But it isn't."

He sat down on the floor near the chair. "Look," he said. "I've been thinking about your room. Yours and Margot's."

Moira looked surprised—and then pleased. "You have?" she asked. She dropped her book and scooted forward in the chair. "What about our room?"

"Well, I was thinking about how Margot likes to keep everything sort of . . . well, organized, and you . . ." He stopped, trying to think of a good way to put it.

"And I'm messy." Moira squeezed her big dark eyes into angry slits. "I like being messy. Being neat is boring. I hate people who are neat."

Rudy didn't want an argument. "Okay, okay," he said. "But I just thought of a way to help you and Margot stop fighting so much. What I thought was, it's no wonder you and Margot can't get along. You're just too different to have to share a room. What I thought was maybe Mom could clean out that little room next to hers and one of you could move in there."

Moira stared at Rudy. "No," she said quickly and definitely. "I don't want to have my own room." Her eyes were wide again, almost frightened-looking.

"Why not?" Rudy said. "Just think about it. You could have your stuff all over—"

"No. No, I don't want to." Moira's eyes were huge and her voice sounded shaky. "I don't like to sleep in an empty room. I don't like to wake up and nobody's there. When I wake up and nobody's there I think they've all gone away. I think everybody's gone away."

Margot came in then and the conversation stopped, but Rudy had some interesting things to think about. That night in bed he went over the things Moira had said, particularly the part about everybody going away. That was when it occurred to him that maybe Moira was afraid that everyone would go away—*like Art had done.*

He'd never thought much about how Art's skipping out had affected the M and M's. He knew how it had affected him. Not much, except for a general feeling of relief. But then, Art had only been his stepfather and he'd always made it pretty clear that stepfathering wasn't a job he had much interest in. As far as Rudy could remember, he hadn't been the greatest as a real father either, but he did have spells of being really nice to the girls. Rudy could remember him bringing them presents and carrying them around the yard on his shoulders when he was in a good mood.

Just before he went to sleep Rudy remembered

that Moira was about six years old when Art bailed out. So maybe if one parent walks out on you at that age you might just be afraid that other people might do the same thing. Irrationally afraid, maybe. Almost like a phobia. It was a possibility, he decided, that needed a little more research.

Chapter 12

ON SUNDAY MORNING, Heather phoned to say that Barney had moved her next riding lesson up to Monday.

"Monday's all right with you, isn't it?" she asked. "You said you didn't baby-sit on Mondays and Tuesdays, didn't you?"

As a matter of fact, it was great. Heather hadn't mentioned old Styler one way or the other, but Rudy couldn't imagine him having the nerve to show up again at the scene of the great hedge-sitting demonstration. So the next riding lesson would almost certainly be Ty-less, and the sooner was probably the better, before Ty got over his punctures and embarrassment.

"Right," Rudy said. "That's fine. Monday's fine with me."

But when Monday morning came and Heather and Rudy rounded the curve above the ranch, it was immediately clear that something unusual was going on. A dust cloud hovered over the corral area, several extra cars were parked near the house, and Jeb and Angela's big red-and-silver horse trailer was pulled up near the stock barn. While Heather was parking the car Barney came out to meet them.

"Hey, Barn. What's up?" Rudy said as he got out of the car.

Barney shrugged. "Wouldn't you know it. My mom and dad got home early and Granddad decided to do a quick roundup while my dad is here to help. I didn't know about it till this morning or I'd have called."

"Roundup? In June?" Rudy asked.

"Yeah," Barney said. "A vetting thing. Doc Mayberry says there's been some blackleg going around and he thinks we ought to get the new calves vaccinated right away. And they're going to be checking for sticker-eye and that sort of thing too. Seems like the stickers are especially bad this year."

Rudy knew about blackleg, a deadly cattle disease that usually attacked young stock. But knowing how important it was to keep a herd healthy didn't make the whole thing any less disappointing. "Guess that means we won't be able to ride today?" he said, trying not to sound too unhappy.

Heather's smile had disappeared and when it came back it looked a little bit forced. "Well, that's all right," she said. "Maybe next week we can—"

"No, today's all right," Barney broke in. "We just

126

won't be able to ride in the arena. They're using it as a cutting pen. But we can take a trail ride. Granddad and Wade got the home range stock in already and Granddad says the three of us can bring in the cows and calves from Tumbleweed Hill while they get started on the others."

Heather's smile went from counterfeit to authentic in a split second. "You mean we're going to get to help with a roundup?" she asked.

Barney grinned. "That okay with you?"

"Wow," Heather said, "it's fabulous. That is, if you think I'm ready for it."

"Nothing much to it," Barney said. "Applesauce knows what to do. And you can just keep the herd moving while Rudy and I bring in the stragglers."

It was all right with Rudy too. A ride in the country with Barney and Heather—and no Styler—was even better than all right.

"Okay, cowpokes," he said, hitching up his pants and doing his Windy Dayes squint. "Let's go git them little dogies."

In the barnyard, Applesauce, Bluebell, and Badger were already waiting at the hitching rack. All three of them were acting a little jazzed up, moving around restlessly, tossing their heads and pawing the earth.

"Why are they fussing around like that?" Heather asked. "They seem to be nervous or something."

Barney stopped tightening Badger's cinch. "Well, they're just excited, I guess." He nodded in the direction of the corrals from where the sounds of hoofbeats, bellowing cows, and bawling calves could be heard. "They want to get in on the act."

"Well, I don't blame them," Heather said. "I'm excited too."

Barney gave another tug on the cinch strap and then suddenly hit Badger sharply in the ribs with his open hand. Then he tightened the cinch again.

"Why'd he do that?" Heather whispered indignantly to Rudy. "Why did he slap Badger like that?"

"Just meanness, I guess," Rudy said, but then he grinned. "No, that didn't hurt Badger. Just surprised him enough to make him stop blowing himself up. Some horses do that while you're saddling them, so the cinch won't be so tight when they let out the air. But then the saddle's too loose. So you have to give them something else to think about so they'll deflate."

Heather sighed and shook her head. "There's a lot more to this horsemanship business than I expected. You and Barney are really experts." She looked at Rudy admiringly and he did an "aw shucks" expression and said, "Barney's the expert." But it did make him feel good.

The horses were almost ready to go when Barney's father came out of the arena on Dynamo. Jeb Crookshank was wearing fringed leather chaps and a wide belt with a big silver buckle, and looked like something a mad scientist might have put together out of the best-looking parts of half a dozen Hollywood cowboys.

"Pyramid Hill's Marlboro Man," Rudy whispered to Heather. "That's what Natasha calls him."

Heather laughed. "I know," she whispered back. "I've heard her on the subject of Jeb Crookshank. I guess she never was too crazy about him even when they were in high school together and he was the number one big man on campus—and *knew* it."

"Right," Rudy said. "A world-class ego, she says. And besides—"

He was going to go on to say something about how Natasha held it against Jeb that he'd always been too busy being a rodeo star to have much time for Barney, but about then Jeb finished latching the gate and suddenly spurred Dynamo into a racehorse gallop straight at them. He blasted full speed across the barnyard and pulled up so sharply, the big bay almost sat down on his haunches.

Rudy smiled inwardly. Charlie and Jeb Crookshank were definitely not "like father, like son." One of Charlie's strict rules was that you never pushed your cow pony any more than necessary. You didn't gallop when a trot would do just as well, and you never ran full-out unless you were chasing something. That kind of show-off riding was what Charlie called "ginning around," and if you were a kid it could get you grounded. Jeb had undoubtedly been raised to know that a full-out run across the barnyard was definitely "ginning around," but now that he was a big rodeo star no one was going to ground him. Not even his father.

"Rudy," Jeb said with his Marlboro Man smile—a wide gully of white teeth across a rugged sun-browned landscape. "Good to see you. And"—he paused and did an exaggerated double take—"Heather Hanrahan?" he asked. "Well, well. You've done some growing up since I last saw you." That was all he said with words, but he was definitely making his face say a lot more.

The kinds of things that someone her own age—or younger—couldn't say to Heather without getting a taste of her "ice princess" number. She was beginning to frown when Barney came to the rescue.

"Dad," he said, "Granddad said we were to round up the Tumbleweed Hill stock and bring them in right away. So I guess we'd better get going."

Jeb let them go then, but he insisted on getting off Dynamo to help Heather into the saddle, getting in a few more embarrassing comments as he did, and another one or two as they started out of the yard. By the time they were finally underway Rudy was thinking that there were some occasions when having a father was every bit as embarrassing as not having one, if not more so.

The trail to Tumbleweed acreage went across the rolling hills of the home pasture and then down into a valley and up the other side. They had to ride single file on the narrower trails, so it wasn't easy to talk, but that didn't matter. It was great anyway, all the familiar sights and sounds and smells: the sun on your head and back, the changing views of grassy slopes and wooded valleys, the smell of horse and hillside, the easy rhythmic motion, the clop of hooves, the squeak of leather.

Up ahead Barney, on Badger, led the way at a fast walk, with Heather close behind on Applesauce. Rudy brought up the rear on Bluebell, trotting now and then to keep up, but mostly just ambling along daydreaming and enjoying the ride. Daydreaming about someday owning a big ranch like the Crooked Bar—after becoming a rich and famous actor and comedian, of course.

Later, when they reached the valley, the three of them rode side by side and Heather asked a lot of questions about the ranch and the different kinds of stock that Charlie raised.

"Most of the cattle in the arena this morning looked pretty much the same," she said. "Brown and white with woolly-looking faces. They're Herefords, aren't they?"

Barney looked surprised and pleased that Heather knew about Herefords. "Right," he said. "Herefords. Most of the cattle on the ranch are Herefords, but Granddad runs some Brahmans and even a few long-horns. Rodeo stock mostly. You'll get to see some of them today. A lot of the rodeo stock is on the Tumble-weed pasture."

Heather, it seemed, knew something about Brahmans too. "I've seen them in rodeos," she said. "They're the huge ones with the humped backs, aren't they? The ones they use in the bull riding contests?"

"Yeah," Barney said. "Those are Brahman bulls."

Heather was quiet for a minute, and then she said, "They looked terribly—well, dangerous. Are they? Dangerous, I mean?"

Rudy got the picture. "No," he said, catching Barney's eye and grinning. "The ones we'll be rounding up today will be cows and calves. Cows aren't danger-ous, are they, Barney?"

"No," Barney said. "Cows aren't dangerous." But then after a minute he added, "Not unless they think you're trying to hurt their calves."

That was all that was said about cows with calves at the time, but it was only a little later that the subject

131

came up again. They had just reached the east fence of the Tumbleweed acreage and were about to fan out and start driving the cattle down to the home pasture. From where they had stopped to breathe their horses after the climb, they could look down and see several small groups of cows and calves sprinkled here and there over the hillside.

"But that's not all of them," Barney said. "There's got to be a bunch more in the brush over in the gully there. I'll go that way. And Rudy, you go to the left past the spring. And Heather, you go straight back down the way we came. Pick up that bunch we just came past. Just set Applesauce toward them and she'll take care of it. Don't hurry them. Just keep them moving along slowly. And we'll be meeting you with some others down there where the hill flattens out. Got it?"

"Got it," Rudy and Heather said in unison. Heather looked sky-high with excitement, and Rudy wasn't exactly feeling bored either.

"Okay," Barney said. "Let's go." He was already turning Badger to the right when he suddenly pulled up. "Listen," he said. Then Rudy heard it too. From somewhere down toward the spring a calf was bawling. As they listened the weak, hoarse cry came again and then again. "Something's wrong," Barney said. "Come on." He started down the hill with Rudy and Heather following close behind.

The Tumbleweed spring was near the bottom of a narrow valley where water trickled out of a sharp rocky cliff and fell, in a thin waterfall, into a small lake below. Above and on both sides the lake was surrounded by steep and heavily wooded banks, so the only approach to the water's edge was on the downhill slope. There, a deeply worn cattle trail led through a mud flat and down to the water's edge. The mud, constantly churned by many hooves, was black and deep and squishy and smelled of cow manure and stagnant water.

They found the calf at the edge of the pond where the earth under an oak tree had been washed away on one side, leaving a network of exposed roots arching down into the mud below. The calf, a very young Brahman, had a front leg caught in among the roots. Its other front leg was bent backward and its head hung down over the trapped leg. Now and then it raised its head, bawled weakly, and then collapsed again. Barney reined Badger to a stop at the edge of the muddy area and Rudy and Heather pulled up beside him.

"Oh, the poor little thing," Heather said. "Do you suppose its leg is broken?"

"Not broken. Stuck though," Barney said, sounding like his granddad. When things got critical Barney always sounded like his granddad.

Rudy urged Bluebell a few steps forward into the deep mud.

"Hold it, Rudy," Barney said. "And be quiet." Rudy pulled up and they sat quietly listening. There was no sound except for an occasional weak cry from the calf. Barney twisted in the saddle looking around the banks of the pond and then down the trail. At last he said, "All right. The cow must have given up and gone off. Come on, Rudy. We'll get her loose." He swung down, dropping the reins over Badger's head so that he would stand still.

"Wait a minute," Rudy began. "Maybe we ought to look around a little more first and—"

Barney stopped and looked back, and Rudy shut up. He'd seen that look on Barney's face before and he knew that there was no use arguing. When Barney got that gleam in his eye there were only two choices—to chicken out or to yell "Geronimo" and jump. Rudy took a deep breath, looked around one more time, got down off Bluebell, and waded out into the mud.

The little heifer's leg was wedged in tightly between two thick roots. It looked a little bit swollen, and every time they tried to pry it loose she struggled and bawled with surprising strength and volume. But at last one root began to give, the space widened, and the leg came free. They had just managed to carry the calf back a few feet from the bank when a very big, very angry Brahman cow came out of the brush below the spring.

Rudy and Barney were steadying the heifer as she started to walk, using her swollen leg gingerly, when they heard Heather shout, "Look out." And there the cow was, charging straight at them.

They ran in different directions. Instinct must have taken over and Barney's instinct, as a born-and-bred cowboy, must have been to get to the horses. He ran up the hill while Rudy ran back through the mud toward the oak trees.

Barney might have made it to Badger, except that the shouting and the charging cow was too much for the horses' training, and reins down or not, they bolted. Heather and Applesauce had started up the hill too. It was entirely Applesauce's decision. "I didn't

134

tell her to," Heather said later. "I was just sitting there paralyzed by fear." So Heather and the horses went up the hill and Rudy went up a tree. And Barney was left all alone out on the open hillside.

Rudy's oak tree was an easy climb, with lots of low horizontal branches, and he'd reached a fairly high limb when he looked down and saw what was happening. The cow had stopped near her calf and was swinging her big horned head from side to side. Then she let out a bellow and started full speed toward Barney. Without waiting to get his balance Rudy bailed out and lit flat on his backside in the mud.

"Run, Barney. Run!" Rudy screamed and, jumping to his feet, started running toward the calf, waving his arms and yelling, "Here, cow. Here, cow. Come and get me." When the cow stopped and turned in his direction Rudy came to a stop too. It wasn't until she started in his direction that he whirled around and plowed back through the mud toward the oak. He got to the tree with the cow not far behind him and, in spite of muddy hands and feet, went up it like a squirrel.

For a moment the cow stared up at him, snorting and pawing the mud before she turned away and trotted back toward her calf. Fifty yards up the hill, Barney had almost reached the horses when Badger snorted and whirled away. Holding his head sideways to avoid stepping on his reins, he trotted on up the hill, leaving Barney still stranded out in the open. Rudy was watching from his tree as the cow spotted Barney and again started after him. Rudy jumped out of the tree for the second time. He made a little better landing, more or less on his feet this time, but then lost his balance and sprawled forward flat on his belly in the stinking mud.

It wasn't until the cow had turned back once more to chase Rudy up the tree that Barney caught up with Badger, and the "Terminator Cow" episode finally came to an end.

The rest of the day was something of an anticlimax. The little heifer got her legs in working order, she and her mother joined the other cattle, and the roundup continued as planned. Except that Rudy had to do his part while wearing a fairly thick layer of mud and smelling like something that should have been buried a month ago.

He must have looked terrible too. Bad enough to scare horses, at least, because the first time he tried to get back on Bluebell she took one look and did one of her famous sideways jumps. It took quite a lot of soft talk before she would let him get close enough to get back in the saddle.

After the scare had worn off and they'd all calmed down a little, the three of them did a lot of laughing. "Here, cow. Here, cow," one of them would say and they'd all go into hysterics. Not to mention what happened every time the others got close enough to Rudy to smell him. Rudy laughed too. He felt a lot like laughing the rest of the day—in spite of the smell.

Chapter 13

HE WAS A HERO. He hadn't thought about it that way at the time. He had just seen what was about to happen to Barney and he'd done what was necessary without stopping to think about it. But that, according to Heather, was what made it heroic. And Heather wasn't the only one to say so.

Barney said it, too, in a different way. Right after they'd gotten back on their horses and convinced the man-killer cow to call off the war, Barney had ridden up beside Rudy. "Hey, thanks," he said. "Thanks a lot, old buddy." And then he stuck out his hand and shook Rudy's, smelly mud and all. That was all he said in words, but, knowing Barney, Rudy was able to read a lot more between the lines.

And later, when they got back to the ranch, Charlie had a few words to say on the subject. Quite a lot of words actually, considering the fact that Charlie Crookshank sometimes got by for days at a time on about half a dozen syllables. Charlie made his lengthy comments after he'd ridden out on his old buckskin to help get the Tumbleweed stock into one of the holding corrals.

As soon as he got a good look at Rudy, he did his slow, lopsided grin and asked, "Git throwed?"

"Well, no," Rudy said. "I jumped, actually." And then Barney and Heather took over and told Charlie the whole story and that's when Charlie really got wordy. He began by getting on Barney for trying to work with a calf without knowing exactly where its mother was.

"You know better'n that, Barney," he said. But then he turned to Rudy and said, "Handled yourself real well, pardner. Right proud of you." Then he looked Rudy over some more before he started up his grin again. "Go on in and wash up some. Can't get in this young lady's new car thataway."

Heather laughed. "Thanks, Mr. Crookshank," she said. "That little problem had occurred to me. All that gunk on my new upholstery."

So they went inside, and the first thing they had to do was tell the whole story over again for Barney's mother.

Angela Crookshank was wearing one of her Indian outfits, a low-cut velvet blouse over a full skirt with a heavy turquoise-and-silver belt around her narrow waist. She laughed when she saw Rudy. He'd noticed before how glamorous Angela looked when she put her hands on her hips, tossed her long blond hair, and laughed. He'd seen her do the same thing at rodeos when she'd finished a barrel race or a stunt-riding demonstration. Seen her get off her horse, lead it up in front of the judges' stand, bow and make her horse bow too—and then she'd laugh, with her head thrown back and her hair blowing in the wind while the crowd roared and clapped.

There wasn't any roaring crowd in the ranch house kitchen, but Angela did the head-tossing laugh anyway when they finished telling about what happened. And then, still laughing, she said, "Rudy, you are just *too* much! How do you always manage to be the fall guy?"

When Rudy was in Barney's bathroom, taking a shower and getting into some borrowed clothing, it occurred to him what Angela hadn't mentioned. What Angela hadn't said anything about was that Barney could have been killed. She didn't seem to have noticed that part of it at all.

On the way home in the Toyota, Heather said, "You know what you were like? You were just like those rodeo clowns. You know, during the bull-riding events when the clowns keep the bulls from attacking the riders who fall off. You know, risking your neck to get the bull's attention—okay, it was only a cow, but you were risking your neck just the same."

"Thanks a lot," Rudy said. "That's what I like to hear. Rudy the clown."

Heather laughed. "No. That's not the point. I didn't mean you were a clown. What I meant was that what you did took lots of guts. And what the clowns do takes a lot of courage. I've always thought that the clowns have to be the bravest ones in the whole rodeo. Don't you think so?"

Rudy hadn't thought much about rating rodeo bravery before, but when he did he had to agree. Lying in bed that night, he went over the whole thing again and decided that what Heather said was true. For one thing what the clowns did was really dangerous, there was no doubt about that. He'd often seen them in action at local rodeos and on TV, too, climbing fences or jumping into barrels with huge angry bulls about two steps behind them. And what he'd done *had* been very similar. So maybe he wasn't so chicken after all. And now, maybe, no matter what might happen in the future, people wouldn't forget that he hadn't been chicken when the cow attacked Barney. Barney, in particular, wouldn't forget. It was a good thought to go to sleep on.

The next day, Tuesday, Natasha went to Jackson to go shopping and visit some friends. She took the M and M's with her, so Rudy had the whole day to himself and no plans. So right away he called up Barney to suggest that he could help again with the roundup.

"All done. Finished last night," Barney said in a kind of excited, upbeat tone of voice. Rudy could almost see his wide Crookshank grin. "Hey, guess what?" he went on. "I'm going to go to Montana next week with my mom and dad—to a couple of rodeos. And I might even get to compete in some of the junior events. My dad just told me today."

"Wow," Rudy said. "That's great. Fantastic. Amazing." It really was pretty amazing, because it almost never happened anymore. When Barney was a little kid Jeb and Angela had taken him with them once in a while when they went on the rodeo circuit. But he hadn't gotten to go at all for a long time. Barney said it was because his folks didn't want him to miss school, but Rudy had noticed he didn't get to go during summer vacations either.

"Fantastic," Rudy said again. "How long will you be gone?"

"Oh, for a week or so," Rudy said. "But we don't leave until Friday, so today is okay. I could come to your place. Granddad's got some Cattlemen's Association stuff to do in town and I could ride in with him."

"Hey," Rudy said. "Great! We could go skateboarding at the school, or hang out downtown, or—hey, it's going to be real hot. I could call Julie and see if we can go swimming in her pool. Okay?"

"Sure," Barney said. "Whatever."

Whatever. Barney used to say "whatever" a lot when they were discussing what to do with some free time, but it was a word that Rudy hadn't heard much of recently. "Whatever" sounded like the old Barney.

Rudy hung up the phone and leaned against the kitchen sink thinking—and grinning. He didn't realize how hard he was grinning until he caught sight of himself in Natasha's broom closet mirror. Not cool, he thought. Pretty sappy-looking, actually. But he didn't care. Grabbing the flyswatter off the windowsill and waving it like a baton, he did a kind of drum major strut around the kitchen table before he came back to the phone and called Julie Harmon.

Julie sounded pleased when she found out it was

Rudy on the phone. "Well, hi, Rudy Drummond," she said. "It is Rudy, isn't it? Not Windy Dayes. Or Miss Harrington?" Miss Harrington was the principal at Pyramid Hill's Middle School and one of the people Rudy was especially good at imitating.

Putting on his creaky "Miss Harrington" voice, Rudy said, "Well, actually, I'm calling to speak to your parents about your perfectly terrible grades, young lady." Julie shrieked with laughter. Julie was always an easy audience. But then Rudy got down to business. "No, you were right the first time. It's Rudy. I was just wondering . . . well, it *is* a very hot day, isn't it?"

"Oh, I get it," Julie said. "You want to go swimming, right?

"Swimming?" Rudy pretended surprise. "What a great idea, now that you mention it. But now that you mention it, Barney's going to be in town today and maybe he and I—"

"Barney!" Julie shrieked. Then she put her hand over the receiver and shrieked a lot of other stuff that Rudy couldn't quite hear. When she came back on the phone he found out that she'd been talking to Jennie and Stephanie, who were spending the whole day at the Harmons'.

"Some other kids might be coming later too," Julie said. "So you and Barney come anytime. Come anytime—as soon as Barney gets there."

It was one of the all-time great afternoons. Stephanie was wearing a killer bikini bathing suit and looking even more sensational than usual. Two more guys and another girl showed up, so they had enough people for a major-effort game of water polo. Barney was the big star, as usual, and made all the goals, and got all kinds of attention, especially from the girls. But Rudy got lots of attention, too, because people kept asking him to do his impersonation of Michael Jackson —the one he'd done for the graduation assembly. Around four o'clock Julie fixed tuna sandwiches and popcorn, and just before the party broke up Stephanie actually spoke to Rudy without his having to start the conversation, which was practically a first. He came up out of the pool near where she was sitting and before he even opened his mouth she said, "Would you mind standing somewhere else? You're dripping on me." It wasn't much, maybe, but along with everything else it made it a perfect day.

Perfect at least in most respects. The only thing that might have made it better would have been if he and Barney had more time to talk, if he could have found out, for instance, just where the gold-mining scheme stood at the moment and if Tyler's hedge-sitting fiasco had really changed Barney's feelings about the whole picture. But Barney had gone straight downtown from the Harmons' to meet his granddad at the Cattlemen's Association building, and Rudy walked home alone.

Natasha wasn't back yet when Rudy got home, so he fixed himself a peanut butter sandwich and turned on the TV. But nothing very interesting was on. Nothing, at least, as interesting as thinking about what a great day it had been. So he shut off the tube—and it was at that point he hit on the idea of having another session with *Conquering Your Fears.*

As he got the book out from under his mattress he

was feeling pretty confident that he was certainly going to be much more successful with the phobia treatments than he'd been before. After all, if a person could keep his cool in a situation like the killer-cow episode, he surely wouldn't hit the panic button over imagining something scary, or maybe crawling into a little old closet. Or even, for that matter, a deserted gold mine. Like the book said, some phobias were simply outgrown as a person matured.

But when he tried the "implosion" method he nearly went into shock, and he couldn't get into the hall closet any farther than his ankles. Not without getting a distinct impression that if he pushed it anymore somebody would have to scrape him off the ceiling. The whole thing was a major disappointment, and after being so up all afternoon it was particularly hard to take.

He was still feeling the letdown that evening, and even though he was trying to hide it Natasha must have noticed. Sometimes, when she wasn't too busy or tired, Natasha seemed to have a built-in mood detector. They were cleaning up after dinner when she suddenly said, "Is something wrong, Rudy? I'm getting a feeling that all is not well."

"Wrong?" He gave her a big "can't imagine what you're talking about" number. "No. Everything's fine as far as I know. Have you checked the evening news? Maybe World War Three has started."

"Very funny," Natasha said. "I just meant that you seem a little bit gloomy."

"I'm fine," Rudy said. "I had a terrific day, actually. One of the best." He'd already told Natasha a little about the swimming party at the Harmons'. "It was a blast at Julie's. Oh, yeah, I forgot to tell you about something. Barney's going to get to go to a couple of rodeos in Montana with Jeb and Angela."

"Oh, really." Natasha looked surprised. "I thought they didn't take him with them anymore."

"Well, they don't very much. Not during school anyway."

"And not much in the summer either." Natasha's lip curled up on one side the way it always did when she was talking about something that made her angry. "Not since he's gotten to be so embarrassingly grown-up looking."

Rudy halfway knew what she meant, but he asked anyway. "What do you mean embarrassing?"

"Embarrassing to his glamorous parents. Angela probably hates having a great big teenaged son around. Makes her look too old. And Jeb, too, for that matter. Jeb probably doesn't like being reminded that he's getting pretty old for rodeo competition."

Rudy knew how Natasha had always felt about Jeb and Angela. "Yeah," he said. "I know. You think they always go off and leave him too much. But Charlie was always there and Belle, too, until—well, until she died. It's not like his folks just went off and left him alone. And Barney never seemed to mind about their being gone. At least he never said anything about it to me."

Natasha stopped wiping out the sink and turned to give Rudy a long, slow look. "No," she said finally. "Barney probably wouldn't have said anything. He's not one to talk about his personal problems very much, is he?"

"Problems?" Rudy said. "What problems?"

Natasha sighed impatiently. "I know you've always thought that Barney is the next thing to superhuman, but he isn't, you know. His grandmother used to worry about him a lot. She used to tell me—" She stopped and stared down at her hands for a minute before she turned toward Rudy again.

Rudy grinned sarcastically, letting his expression say that he found the whole idea of Barney having serious problems pretty funny. "Well, go on. What did Belle tell you?"

"Well, all right." Natasha was getting angry. "I never said anything to you because Belle wouldn't have wanted me to. But she and I used to talk a lot on the phone and she told me about these terrible anxiety attacks Barney used to have, so bad that sometimes he wouldn't be able to go to sleep at night. He'd be wide awake until morning and then he'd fall asleep at school or even at the table at dinnertime."

"Yeah," Rudy said, grinning. "I remember about him going to sleep at school. But it just seemed like, well, you know, like part of his supercool personality. Everybody thought so. People used to think it was great to be so relaxed—about school and everything. Some of the other guys even used to pretend that they were asleep, too, because all the girls seemed to think it was so cute when Barney did it."

"Well, Belle didn't take it so lightly," Natasha said. "It really worried her. She thought it was because Jeb and Angela were away so much and never paid a great deal of attention to Barney even when they were home. She said it was usually when Jeb and Angela were away that Barney stayed awake all night—listening for them to come home."

Rudy found it hard to believe. It just didn't fit, any of it. Barney—supercool, unflappable Barney—lying awake nights worrying? It just didn't seem possible. Rudy was still trying to make some sense of what Natasha had said when he tuned back in to what she was still saying.

"And then there was the way he always pushed himself to do dangerous things," Natasha said, and Rudy's attention really went on alert.

"Barney? Pushed himself?" he asked.

"Yes. You know how you boys were always doing stunts that usually didn't turn out too well"—she smiled ruefully—"especially for you. And I always thought you were both responsible. You know, kind of egging each other on. But Belle felt it was part of a pattern for Barney. She thought it was because his parents, particularly Jeb, did dangerous things all the time, like riding broncs and bulldogging, and that Barney felt he had to constantly prove he was just as brave and daring as Jeb was in order to earn their approval. Barney kept promising Belle it wouldn't happen again, and you promised, too, remember? And then it would. Not the same stunt, but something just as risky. And I don't suppose Belle and I even heard about a lot of the crazy things you kids did."

"Yeah, I guess you didn't," Rudy said, with his mind only halfway on what he was saying—because the other half was too busy thinking. Thinking, yeah, maybe she's right. Maybe Natasha and Belle were right. Maybe that explained a lot of things.

"Wow!" he said finally.

"Wow?"

"Yeah, wow. It's just that I never . . . I never thought about . . ." Rudy hung up his dish towel, put away the frying pan, and started out of the room.

"Rudy?" Natasha's voice squeezed into his consciousness, but he just kind of waved his hand back at her and kept on going. He had to get to his room where he could be alone and do some heavy thinking.

Collapsed on his bed with his arms behind his head, Rudy let his mind go over and around and through the middle of all the unbelievable stuff Natasha had said. And the more he thought about it the more believable it all became. There was, for instance, the way Barney used to react to any mention of his sleep sessions in class. Even though he must have realized that no one else took it seriously, except maybe the teachers, Barney had been very sensitive about it. It hadn't paid for anyone to tease him about it.

And then there were the dangerous games. Looking back, Rudy remembered how Barney's whole personality seemed to change when one of his "highly fatal" projects was about to happen. Like when he thought up the swing across Wild Horse Gulch or one of his other daredevil schemes—and the good old "whatever" Barney would disappear and it was no use even to think of arguing with the stranger that was left behind.

So that was what Natasha had meant the other night when she said "poor little Barney." She meant that lucky old good-looking, popular Barney had a problem too. A serious one. Not a phobia, perhaps, but on second thought it was very like a phobia, because it also had to do with fear. A terrible "excessive and inappropriate" fear that his beautiful, glamorous parents were about to dump him for good.

The concept took a lot of getting used to. Rudy was still getting used to it a lot later when a new and even more mind-boggling idea occurred to him: Maybe looking for gold in the old mine was just one more example of Barney's powerful need to prove that he was as daring and heroic as his rodeo star parents.

Rudy was halfway out of the room on his way to the telephone in the kitchen before he realized that it was much too late to be calling the Crooked Bar Ranch, and that the whole subject was not the sort of thing that one discussed on the telephone. In fact, it was not the sort of subject that one discussed at all without giving the matter a lot of careful thought.

Rudy got back into bed and started on the careful thinking.

Chapter 14

Rudy spent a lot of time that night thinking about what he wanted to say to Barney. But on Wednesday morning when they did talk on the phone, Barney was too busy practicing roping to say much at all.

"Hey, Rudy-dudey." Barney sounded excited, almost breathless. "I've been working on my roping since seven o'clock and I'm getting a lot better. My dad says I'm better than most of the kids he's seen competing in the junior events. Why don't you come on out and watch?"

But since Rudy had to baby-sit in the afternoon there really wasn't time. Thursday was pretty much the same, a slightly longer phone conversation in the morning, mostly about roping and calf riding, and that was all. And on Friday, Barney left for Montana. But by then Rudy had almost decided not to talk to Barney about the things that Natasha had said, anyway.

The more he thought about it, the more he realized how hard it would be to discuss really personal things with Barney. Things like what bad parents Jeb and Angela had always been, and about how Barney only wanted to do the gold-mining thing, as well as a lot of other dangerous or even illegal stuff, because he needed to feel as brave and daring as his famous parents. It was really hard even to imagine bringing up embarrassing things like that with a person like Barney.

And there was another reason, too, that Rudy was glad to put off mentioning any of it to Barney—it really was beginning to look like it might not be necessary. It just might be that the Pritchard's Hole problem had solved itself. Of course, Rudy hadn't come right out and asked, but Barney hadn't so much as mentioned the gold mining, or Tyler Lewis, when they were together on Tuesday, or later on the phone. Not a word. It was as if he was so excited about going on the rodeo circuit that he'd lost all interest in anything else. Maybe being with his parents in Montana and getting to compete in the rodeo was giving him enough of a chance to prove whatever it was he needed to prove to himself. Enough for one summer anyway. It would be great if that turned out to be true.

There was, of course, one bit of good news that was definitely true. Whatever was, or was not, going to happen at Pritchard's Hole wasn't going to be happening very soon. Nothing to worry about for a week or so, at least.

But that left Rudy with a lot of mornings of fooling around the house or hanging out downtown and maybe a visit or two to the Harmons' swimming pool, where Stephanie Freeman just might be, too, if he was lucky. And afternoons of baby-sitting his sisters. It didn't sound great, perhaps, but it could be worse. A lot worse.

As for the baby-sitting, it was continuing to be a little less boring since he'd begun his research project on the M and Ms' personalities. One of the subjects he was most interested in was what kind of things they fought about and who usually started it. Before his research project he'd never thought much about who started it. There didn't seem to be any point in asking, since they both always claimed the other one had. He'd always assumed that it was mostly Margot's fault, because it was Moira who usually wound up with the most scratches and bites and bruises. But when he started really watching he began to see a kind of pattern to most of their fights.

Like the one, for instance, about the new pink tutu. They'd both wanted the pink one, but Natasha had given it to Margot since it was, it seemed, her turn to have firsties. Moira had claimed that the new tutu was too small around the middle for chubby old Margot, but apparently Natasha hadn't agreed.

The fight began on Friday at the exercise barre when Moira noticed—or said she did, Rudy hadn't been able to see it—a tiny hole in the seam near the back zipper of the pink tutu.

"Margot's torn her tutu," Moira said.

Rudy looked up from his book. He'd pulled the overstuffed chair into the studio so that he could read and still keep one eye on the girls' dance practice.

"Where?" he said.

"Where? Where? Where?" Margot said, practically tying herself in a knot to see the place on the back of her waist where Moira was pointing.

"Right there," Moira said. "It's just starting, but it's going to get bigger fast."

"I don't see any hole."

"Well, it's there." Moira's nose was practically touching Margot's back. "It's getting bigger already. Every time you breathe it gets bigger."

"Ruuudy," Margot whined, backing up to Rudy's chair. "Is there a hole in my new tutu?"

"I don't see any hole. Forget about it, both of you, and finish your barre."

So they both went back to the barre, but a minute later Rudy noticed that Moira was whispering a word in between every plié. "Margot's—torn—her—new—tutu."

"Ruuudy. Make her stop," Margot said.

So Rudy did some yelling and Moira stopped whispering. But a little later he noticed that Moira was facing Margot as she did her port de bras, and every time she curved her arms and gracefully bent forward her lips clearly formed the word *"fat!"* He was just opening his mouth to yell when Margot went right from a fifth position into a kind of karate kick that knocked Moira's legs out from under her. By the time he got to them they were rolling on the floor, punching and scratching.

That, he was beginning to realize, was the usual pattern. Margot tended to be pretty cheerful and easygoing most of the time, but when she did finally get mad she *really* lost it. And Moira, on the other hand, never really got angry, except at herself. After she'd teased Margot into a major fit she was always mad at herself, but the next time she had a chance she did it again.

"I hate it when she gets mad like that," Moira told Rudy with tears in her big dark eyes. "I hate it. But then I start teasing her about something and I can't"— she began to sob—"I . . . just . . . can't . . . stop."

"Why can't you stop?" Rudy asked.

"I . . . don't . . . know," Moira wailed. "I . . . just . . . can't . . . stop."

Rudy patted her shoulder. "Well, you can stop crying," he said, "because if you don't stop I'm going to cry too."

Moira went on crying, but with her eyes open— watching to see what Rudy would do. So he threw himself on the floor and began to screech and sob and pound the floor with both fists. It was fun actually, really letting go like that, even though it was only acting. So he kept it up for a while and when he finally did sit up both Moira and Margot were standing over him staring with big round eyes. When he started laughing it took a second before they caught on and laughed too.

So the M and M research had gotten that far into

what they usually fought about. Now, if he could just figure out *why?* And *what would make them stop?*

It was in the early evening after Barney had been gone three or four days, that Rudy got a surprise phone call. From Tyler Lewis, of all people.

"Yo, dude," the all-too-familiar voice said. "Whatcha doing?"

"Styler?" Rudy said, not trusting his own ears.

"You got it. It's the real thing, the stylin' man. I asked you—whatcha doing?"

"Nothing much, actually. Reading a book."

"Reading." Tyler made a snorting noise. "Why don't you come down to Marybelle's. I'm treating. Rotgut for everybody—or whatever."

Marybelle's was the old-fashioned soda fountain on the corner of Main and Nugget. They served great malts and shakes and root beer floats. No rotgut.

"You're treating?"

"Sure. Come join the crowd."

There wasn't any crowd. When Rudy got to the soda fountain Tyler was sitting alone at one of the pink tables. Except for a couple of tourists with some little kids, there was no one else in sight. Tyler was wearing an L.A. Rams football jacket, his usual buckshot jeans, and a pair of pump-up Nikes without any shoelaces. He was drinking a strawberry milk shake and there was another one across the table from him. Rudy sat down and began to drink.

"So," he said after a minute. "What have you been up to lately?"

Ty slurped noisily on his straw. "Not much. Barney's out of town."

"Yeah," Rudy said. "I *know*." He emphasized the *know* to make it say that he didn't need Styler to tell him what Barney was doing.

Tyler's cocky grin said he knew he'd bugged Rudy and he wasn't exactly sorry about it. But after a minute the grin faded, and to Rudy's surprise it was replaced by a weird gloomy expression. At least it looked weird on Styler's face. It suddenly occurred to Rudy that finding out what made Tyler Lewis tick might be another interesting research project—for somebody with a tough skin and a strong stomach, anyway.

"What the hell is there to do in this hick town in the summertime?" Tyler said in a whiny voice. "Nobody's around and there's nothing going on."

"How about Matt and Sky, or Will maybe?"

"Nah," Ty said. "Sky's out of town, too, and Matt and Will are too busy, or something."

Rudy grinned inwardly. Old Styler didn't seem to notice that he had just let it slip that Rudy hadn't just been his second choice as a companion. More like fourth or fifth. Or maybe twentieth, if Styler could think of that many people who might be able to stand his company for a few hours. It didn't bother Rudy much. If you came right down to it, Styler wouldn't have been even his twentieth choice. Besides, he was getting a free milk shake out of it, not to mention a chance to do some research on a particularly peculiar specimen. For one thing, it had occurred to him to wonder why Tyler was so determined to risk his neck finding gold when, as he was always pointing out, his parents were so filthy rich. The answer might be very enlightening.

"So, Styler." Rudy took a big sip of milk shake, wiped off a strawberry-flavored mustache, and started over. "So, what are you planning to do with your part of the loot? You know, from the Pritchard's Hole thing."

Tyler gave him a suspicious look, as if he thought Rudy might be being sarcastic. Rudy did a sincerely interested number that seemed to work, because finally Tyler shrugged and said, "I dunno. Buy some stuff I guess, and put some of it in the bank. Why?"

"Oh, I don't know. I just wondered because, well, it always seems like you can get all the money you want from your parents."

"True." Tyler looked pleased. He always enjoyed a chance to talk about his folks' money. "But, as my dad always says, you can't have too much money. And besides, this will be *my* money, so I'll always have something to fall back on—just in case."

"Just in case?"

"Yeah. In case my dad goes broke again." Tyler suddenly clamped his mouth shut and frowned at Rudy as if he'd said something he hadn't meant to and he was blaming Rudy for it. Rudy tried to look interested but not too interested, and in a minute Tyler went on. "Yeah, my old man, the wheeler-dealer, does that a lot. That's the way it is with real estate. One day you're rich and the next you're"—Tyler paused, shrugged, and then went on—"practically homeless. You ever been practically homeless, Chickie-baby?"

Rudy ignored the "Chickie-baby" and said he guessed not but that he'd like to hear what it was like, and after another suspicious frown Tyler said, "Okay,

I'll tell you. But let's get out of here. You about done with that thing?"

Ty paid up and led the way outside, and while they walked down Main Street he told Rudy all about it. It seemed that Ty's dad had invested in a big new shopping center in L.A., but his partner turned out to be crooked and gypped him out of all the money.

"I mean, all of it," Ty said. "All my old man got was a bunch of tax debts. He even had to sell our house and car to keep from going to jail."

"And you were really . . . homeless?" Rudy asked.

"Well, almost. We lived with my grandmother for a while and then she kicked us out and we moved to this ratty little apartment. And we were just about to get kicked out of that, too, when my dad won this suit against old Vernon—that was his partner's name, Vernon—and we were rich again. But for a long time my dad didn't think we were going to win and if we hadn't it would have been, like, tent city."

"Yeah, well that sounds pretty tough, all right," Rudy said. He meant it too. His family had always been poor, but at least their beat-up old house had been in the family for practically forever, so they'd never had to worry about a place to live. Or about having enemies who were out to get them either, which is what he'd heard about Mr. Lewis. "And then your dad came up here to start his new business because some people back in L.A. were out to get even with him— maybe his old partner, for instance?"

"Well, yeah. Maybe that was a part of it." Ty had a strange look on his face—half embarrassed and half cocky. He was, Rudy could tell, trying to decide whether or not to tell something, so Rudy did his "not-too-interested" bit to keep him from bogging down.

"The other part was because of me. I never told anybody up here because my dad said he'd drill me if I did, but I was in some trouble too. You know—with the man."

"The man?" Rudy said.

"Yeah. You know. The *police.* I got picked up for tagging a couple of times."

"For tagging?"

"You know tagging, don't you?" Ty rolled his eyes in a "I'm being unbelievably patient with this dumb hick" number. "Putting your 'tag' on buses and stuff with spray paint. And then there was this little joyriding thing with a couple of older dudes. Anyway, it's like, one more bust and it's the slammer for old Styler."

Rudy couldn't help gulping a little. "Jail?" he asked.

"Well, juvie, anyway. Juvenile hall. Yeah. One more time, the man said, and it's curtains for Tyler J. Lewis the Third." Ty curled up one side of his mouth in his cocky grin. "Doesn't bother me all that much, but it scares the hell out of my old man." But watching his eyes, Rudy figured that old Styler was a little bit scared too.

That night Rudy went to bed thinking about Ty Lewis and then for a while about Moira and the teasing problem. The whole Pritchard's Hole question, and the claustrophobia research project as well, had pretty much faded to the back of his mind. At least his more or less conscious mind. But it obviously was still there somewhere, because sometime in the middle of the night he had another nightmare. And not a minor-league one either.

This nightmare was big-time—one of the absolute worst. Afterward he realized that if he had told Natasha about it when she came running into the room again, it wouldn't have sounded so horrible. What was so horrible was how clear and plain and real it seemed, and how absolutely panic-stricken he was when he woke up.

The dream was just about being in a room. A small dark room that smelled of dirt. He was sitting in the middle of the room near a smallish table or maybe just a big box. He was feeling kind of good. Kind of big, maybe, and important. And then the noise started, a kind of sliding, scrunching rumble and someone shouting, "Run, Rudy, run." After that there was nothing except a heavy feeling and the smell and taste of dirt and this awful smashing, smothering, endless fear.

But what he told Natasha was that he'd dreamed about the end of the world.

Chapter 15

THE NEXT FEW DAYS were more of the same, except that on Tuesday morning Rudy called up Charlie and arranged for Heather to have another riding lesson—with Rudy as the one and only teacher. They rode mostly in the arena, and near the end of the hour Charlie came out and watched and told Heather she was doing "mighty well." Heather was thrilled. She said that getting a compliment on your horsemanship from Charlie Crookshank was like being told you were a good artist by Michelangelo.

Afternoons, of course, were mostly spent with Moira and Margot, and the only interesting development was a new game the girls were playing. A doll game. Not that their playing dolls was anything new. It was just that Rudy had never noticed them playing this kind of doll game before.

On this particular afternoon he came into the kitchen and noticed that there were a bunch of dolls scattered around on the big oak table. Moira was holding a Barbie and Margot had the Ken doll and they were making the dolls have some kind of conversation. At first Rudy thought it was just your routine Barbie and Ken thing, and he'd started exploring the refrigerator for something to eat when he overheard what Margot was making the Ken doll say—and started to really tune in.

In a phony deep voice Margot was making the Ken doll say, "Hurry up, Natasha. I haven't got all day."

Rudy closed the refrigerator and sat down at the table. "Natasha?" he asked. "Where's Natasha?"

"This is Mom," Moira said, bouncing the Barbie doll up and down.

Rudy pointed at the Ken doll. "And who's that, then?"

"Daddy," Margot said. "This is Daddy."

Rudy was interested right away. The conversation he'd had with Moira about her not liking to be alone had gotten him started thinking about how Art's skipping out had affected Moira and Margot. Neither one of them mentioned Art much anymore, at least not to Rudy. But once, only a few months ago, he'd overheard Moira asking Natasha some questions: Where was Daddy? and When was he going to come back?

"Okay, got it," Rudy said. "That's Art and that is Natasha. And where is Margot—and Moira. And Rudy, too, for that matter. I want to see Rudy."

It turned out that a yellow-headed Dutch doll was supposed to be Margot and the Japanese doll was Moira.

"And Rudy?"

"Well." Moira looked around the table. It was obvious that a Rudy doll hadn't been chosen yet. "Here," she said finally with one of her teasing smiles. "This is Rudy." She held up a troll doll—a short squatty little plastic job with a big nose and lots of green hair.

"Thanks a lot, pal," Rudy said. He took the troll doll and made it bounce the way the girls always did to show that a doll was supposed to be saying something. "Okay, I'm Rudy," he made the troll say. "What are we doing? What's going on here?"

"We're pretending it's Christmas," Moira said. "It's Christmas and we're opening our presents." She picked up the Japanese doll, pushed its arms forward, and made it hold a little plastic mermaid that had come from the top of one of the swizzle sticks Art used to bring home from the 7 Seas Saloon. "Look. I got a beautiful mermaid doll for Christmas. Thank you, Mama and Daddy, for the beautiful doll."

"Don't thank me," Margot made the Ken doll say gruffly. "I wouldn't waste my money on expensive junk like that."

Rudy was surprised. Margot had only been five years old when Art split, but apparently she remembered how Art was always griping about Natasha's spending too much money. But as the game went on it became clear that she remembered Art pretty clearly.

Moira, on the other hand, seemed to be involved in a typically Moira-ish fantasy. In her game she was

making Art and Natasha into some kind of superro-
mantic couple. She had the out-of-focus look in her
eyes that she always got when she was playing one of
her pretend games, and when it was her turn to play
the part of Art she had him saying phony things like,
"Thank you, Natasha darling, for the beautiful wrist-
watch. It's just what I wanted."

It wasn't until Rudy made the troll doll say, "What
did I get for Christmas? Did anybody get a present for
poor old green-haired Rudy?" that Moira's fantasy
world got away from her.

All of a sudden her dreamy smile faded and her
big-eyed face scrunched into a frown. "That's enough
out of you, kid," she said in a mean-sounding voice.
"Shut your big mouth and keep it shut."

It really jolted Rudy, because he remembered Art
saying those very words more than once—whenever
he thought Rudy was getting too much attention. And
it obviously jolted Moira too. She stared at the Ken
doll for a minute as if she really thought the words had
come out of its mouth, and then she looked at Rudy
with a shocked expression on her face.

Just as the game was getting interesting, a neighbor kid came over to get Moira and Margot to go skating, so Rudy didn't get to find out any more about what
the girls remembered about Art and how they felt
about him. But later as he sat on the veranda reading
and watching the skating he was wondering if Moira's
phony memories had anything to do with her teasing
people. Maybe she wasn't admitting to herself how angry she was at Art for skipping out, so the anger had to
come out in other ways and at other people. Perhaps, if

they played the doll family game again, or at least if he could talk to Moira some more, he might find out if his guess was right. And in the meantime, maybe he'd talk to Natasha about it, if she wasn't too tired when she got home.

Only, Natasha seemed pretty tired that night and then, right after dinner, there was another phone call for Rudy.

"Yo, dude," Tyler said when Rudy picked up the receiver. "My folks are out for the evening and there's a lot of beer in the frig. Want to come over and get drunk?"

"Well, I guess not," Rudy said. "Getting drunk makes me destroy things, particularly antiques. The last time I got drunk I smashed a lot of valuable antique chairs. With a sledgehammer. I'm just not to be trusted around beer and French Provincial furniture. Particularly the gilded stuff. The gilded stuff really freaks me out."

"Yeah?" Tyler sounded dubious. "You putting me on?"

"Me? Putting you on? Why would I do a thing like that?"

Tyler's next suggestion was that they go to the video store and try to convince the clerk that they were eighteen so they could rent a porno movie.

"Look, Styler," Rudy told him. "You are obviously still thinking big-city. Everyone in this town knows exactly how old I am, not to mention how old my mother is, and probably how old her mother was. Not to mention what her phone number is in case somebody wanted to call and let her know what I was up to.

165

And most of them probably know who you are by now too. We'd never get away with it."

"Yeah, well, I guess you're right. So, how about going to see *Robin Hood*? My treat."

So they saw *Robin Hood* together, and on Thursday night Rudy actually did go to Tyler's house to watch TV, eat microwave popcorn, and drink his mother's Diet 7-Up. Nobody mentioned beer.

And on the way to the movie, and in between TV shows, Tyler did a lot more talking about things like having money and not having money and what it had been like when his folks lost all theirs. And the terrible things he heard about what happened to people who got sent to juvenile hall. The more Rudy listened the more certain he became that horses weren't the only things bad old Tyler Lewis was scared to death of.

Getting to know Tyler better turned out to have a surprising effect on Rudy. It wasn't that he actually liked the guy more. Not when he knew for certain that things would be right back to normal the minute there was someone else around for Ty to hang out with. He was just that kind of dude—the kind that can't be around two other people without trying to get one of them to help him trash the third guy. So it wasn't so much that he liked him better. It was more—well, it had sort of taken the fun out of hating him. It was, Rudy decided, a lot more fun to hate people you didn't know too much about.

So it turned out to be a very busy and active week, and the only problem with that was that Rudy didn't have much time to work on his own problems. He did get around to trying the "implosion" thing once more without much improvement, and another time he got into the storage closet up to his knees before he started freaking out. But that was about as good as it got.

It was around ten o'clock on Friday morning while Rudy was in the backyard watering Natasha's sweet peas that Murph came out on his back porch and invited Rudy to another chuck wagon breakfast.

"Kind of got carried away on the pancake batter this morning," Murph said as Rudy came up the back steps. "You'd be doing me a big favor if you'd help me eat them up. Hate to have things go to waste."

Good old Murph. Rudy's mouth was watering so much at the thought of Murph's famous pancakes that his drawl gurgled a little while he was doing his usual Windy Dayes response: "Waal, now, pardner. Don't mahnd if ah dew."

The breakfast was terminally delicious, as always, and it wasn't until he'd finished his fourth pancake that they started talking.

"How's your book coming along?" Rudy began by asking, and Murph said "fine" and then went on to talk about a new treatment for agoraphobics that he'd recently heard about. And right after that Rudy surprised himself by saying, "Oh, yeah? That's funny, because I've been reading about treatments for phobias too."

"You have?" Murph pushed back his plate and rested his elbows on the table.

"Yeah. It's really fascinating stuff. I checked out this book that's all about techniques doctors and psychologists have been using to treat people with all kinds of phobias."

167

"Is that so?" Murph said. "Tell me about them."

So Rudy did a long explanation of "implosion" and "progressive challenges" and "attitude readjustment," and Murph listened very carefully with his eyes narrowed and his head nodding slightly from time to time. And when Rudy finally ran down, Murph said, "Yes, fascinating stuff, indeed. And does it work?"

"Work?" Rudy was surprised, but he was careful to sound even more surprised than he actually was. "I guess it does. The book said it worked really well on some patients."

"Yes, but I mean, did it work when you tried it?"

"Oh," Rudy said. "How did you—" He stopped and then decided to come clean—partially anyway. He shrugged. "Yeah, you guessed it. I tried out the 'implosion' thing a little on this problem I have that's sort of like claustrophobia. Not exactly claustrophobia, but I just have this slightly nervous feeling sometimes when I get in a kind of tight place and . . ."

But the more he talked the more certain he became that Murph was waiting for him to tell him the real truth. And then, without even deciding to, he started telling Murph all about the times he'd had the screaming meemies and what had set them off, and the nightmares and how they'd been getting worse lately, and how he'd tried some of the treatments without making much progress. When he finally finished talking his hands felt a little shaky and there was a tightness beginning in his throat.

Murph was still nodding and staring at Rudy with his saggy old eyes looking so intent and focused that

Rudy felt almost hypnotized, like a rabbit caught in the headlights of a car. And then Murph suddenly leaned forward, put his hand on Rudy's arm, and said, "Rudy, tell me. Just how much *do* you remember about being caught in the cave-in?"

Rudy's first reaction was amazement. No acting, no phony amazement. "Cave-in?" he started to say. "What cave-in? I don't remember anything about—" But he hadn't even finished the sentence when something started happening deep inside his head. Little flashes of scenes and sounds and memories, just like when you first wake up and keep getting brief glimpses from a dream before it all fades away. Darkness with a far-off light, strange sounds, creaks and thuds and crashes and muffled voices screaming his name. And then a heavy, smothering, dirty weight on his back and dirt on his face and in his mouth as he tried to scream.

He'd seen it many times before, those same brief frightening flashes, but he'd always thought of them as something left over from a dream. But this time they kept coming, longer and clearer until they began to be tied together, and the next thing he was aware of was being on his feet, pacing the floor with Murph beside him holding him by the shoulders and shaking him hard as they walked up and down the room.

It was Murph's shaking him that finally seemed to help, bringing him back to the present and Murph's kitchen and the taste of maple syrup in his mouth instead of the darkness and the dry, dead taste of sandy earth. At last Murph led him back to his chair and he sank into it. He put his head down on his arms and sat that way for a long time, shuddering so hard his shoulders jumped up and down and his feet jittered around under the chair as if they were trying to dance. It seemed like hours before the shuddering died away enough so that he was able to lift his head and ask Murph to tell him about it.

"You were five, I think," Murph began. "Barney was sick with the measles, so you couldn't go to the Crooked Bar. Natasha was working. It wasn't long before Moira was born, but even so, your mother was working all day and you'd been left at home with your stepfather. But he'd gone off somewhere and left you alone. So I guess you'd gone out looking for someone to play with. And somehow you wound up out by the Jefferson Mine where some older boys were digging a tunnel in the tailings."

"Steve," Rudy said. It came out of nowhere, a name that yesterday he probably wouldn't have remembered, even if someone had mentioned it. Or even a few minutes ago. But now he could almost see him— a big kid, with a broad face and curly dark hair. "It was Steve's clubhouse we were digging. Steve said I could be in the club if I helped dig. Steve . . . Bowles."

"Yes, it was the Bowles boys. Steve and the two younger brothers. Bigger kids than you, all of them, maybe eight to twelve years old. I don't recall the younger boys' names. They moved away from Pyramid soon afterward. I never did find out exactly how it happened, how you happened to be the only one caught when the framing they'd put up inside the tunnel collapsed and then the whole thing caved in. But when it happened the older boys started trying to dig you out while the youngest one ran to get your folks.

But, of course, no one was home at your house and I happened to be out on my veranda . . ."

Rudy was surprised—and relieved—to feel a shaky smile start to curl the corners of his lips. "Studying . . ."

His voice shivered into silence, but Murph grinned and finished it for him. "Yes, studying humanity, quite likely. And so the Bowles boy found me instead and I grabbed a shovel and ran and . . ." He paused and then went on. "There was a big box in the tunnel that probably saved your life."

"The conference table," Rudy said. "Steve called it his conference table."

"No doubt," Murph said. "It appeared that a piece of the framing fell across the box and formed a bit of protection, a pocket of air space, that you had managed to crawl into. When we finally reached you, you seemed to be unconscious, but then you began to cry."

Murph stopped and ran a hand over his eyes and up over his kinky gray hair. "God, I never thought I'd be so glad to hear a kid cry. You cried, screamed really, for a long time. Hung on to me for dear life and buried your face in my jacket and screamed and sobbed and trembled. But by the time I got you back to my house you'd cried yourself to sleep. I put you down on my couch and went over to get Art. He was home by then and I told him what had happened—and what I thought of him for going off and leaving you alone."

Murph stopped and stared over Rudy's head for a while, nodding and then smiling ruefully, until Rudy shook his arm and said, "And then what happened?"

"Well, at first Art, who'd apparently had a beer or

two, threatened to punch me in the face, but then we both calmed down, and I will say that when he came over to look at you—you were still fast asleep—he seemed to suddenly realize what a close thing it had been and he seemed quite shocked and anxious. He begged me not to tell your mother. Said he'd do it himself and that he'd take you to the doctor as soon as you woke up to be sure you were all right. And perhaps he meant to. But then he carried you home—still sleeping —and that was the last I heard about it. Except that the next day he came over and begged me again not to say anything to your mother. He told me that Natasha was in a very emotional state anyway, what with him losing his job, and with the new baby due in just a few weeks—and that there was no point in upsetting her further. And he made a big point of the fact that you'd seemed perfectly normal when you woke up.

" 'He's forgotten all about it,' he kept saying. It seems that when you woke up he told you you'd had a bad dream and then he took you downtown and bought you an ice-cream cone. He kept telling me that when Natasha came home that's all you could talk about—that great big ice-cream cone he bought you. Which didn't surprise me much—considering it was probably the first and only time your stepfather ever bought you anything."

"So, he never told Natasha," Rudy managed to say.

"Apparently not. I suppose when he found out that you'd forgotten the whole event—blocked it out— the temptation not to tell was just too great."

"And you never told her?" Rudy asked.

"No, I never did. She really wasn't feeling well with the baby coming and with all the trouble she and Art had been having, and I just didn't want to give her anything more to worry about. And I'm sure the Bowles boys weren't at all anxious for anyone to know, so apparently they didn't tell anyone either."

"And you never asked me if I remembered? Until today, that is?"

"I did start to once, several years ago. But when I discovered that you really had blocked it out I didn't dare push it. I'd read that the response to reliving a repressed experience can be very dangerous. And I probably wouldn't have had the nerve to tell you today if I'd realized how violent your reaction would be."

"Yeah, violent. Tell me about it," Rudy said, and then grinned. He really was beginning to feel more like himself. Murph poured them some more coffee and Rudy stirred his for quite a while before he said, "I guess the good news is that there's a *good* reason that I keep freaking out in certain situations. I mean, maybe I'm not just your basic nut-case. Or even your basic all-purpose chicken. That's what I used to think it was— general all-purpose chickenhood. Maybe I'm pretty normal after all."

"Better than that," Murph said. "Much better than normal. I mean smarter, and funnier, and more talented, and braver too."

"Aw, shucks," Rudy said, doing an only slightly shaky version of his bashful hillbilly bit. "Knock it off, will ya." But then, as he got up to leave, he added, "And thanks for telling me—about the cave-in and everything." He took a step or two toward the door and

173

stopped and said, "And thanks for the pancakes too."
And just as he was opening the door he turned around
one last time and said, "Oh, yeah. And for saving my
life. Thanks for that too."

Chapter 16

RUDY CAME HOME and collapsed in the hammock on the veranda. Every time he let himself remember the cave-in it came back more and more clearly. All of it. Not just the dreamlike flashes but a clear memory of all of it, right from the beginning. How he'd wandered down Lone Pine and then on out the old road to where the Bowles boys were digging their cave clubhouse. And as he remembered, the shaking came back too. Violently at first but gradually easing as he went over and over and over the worst parts, prying into every faint memory without really wanting to, the way you can't help picking a nasty scab on your knee.

By the time the girls and Ophelia pounded up the steps he was still a little bit shaky, but pretty much back to normal. Maybe not entirely normal, though, because when he told the girls that he wanted them to do their dance practice first and play later, they stared at him for a moment as if they saw something in his face that worried them. And then they did what he said without arguing, which certainly wasn't normal behavior for them.

Collapsed again, this time in the overstuffed chair in the dance studio, he watched his sisters practicing —Moira limbering up at the barre, slim and sleek in her green leotard, and Margot in the famous pink tutu doing chunky pirouettes around the room. And as he watched, his mind went right on rerunning the cave-in. Rerunning it and then, he suddenly realized, putting it into words. Words that needed to be said to somebody. He wanted, he suddenly knew he *needed* to tell somebody all about it. He could feel the words almost like solid things rising up in his throat and for a moment he imagined calling his sisters over and . . . But he stopped himself in time.

It would be way too risky. He had no idea how they would react to such a frightening story, and, to tell the truth, he had no idea how he would react. He didn't want to risk coming completely unglued again —certainly not with Moira and Margot watching. But the need to talk didn't go away.

He managed to get through the afternoon without saying anything, but just barely. And when Natasha finally got home he listened to her stories about what had happened at the store in what he thought was a pretty normal manner. But the need to tell was there in his mind the whole time. And it must have shown, at least a little, because as soon as the girls had gone to bed Natasha as good as brought it up herself. She was on her way into the living room with a cup of coffee when she stopped and turned around.

"Rudy," she said. "What's the matter? Why are you following me around? Is there something you want to tell me?"

"Yeah," he said, feeling the shiver beginning somewhere in the middle of his chest. "I guess there is."

Natasha curled up at one end of the couch and he sat at the other. She stared at him for a moment, puckering her forehead, then she sighed and said, "Okay, shoot. What did they do this time?"

Rudy shook his head. "It's not the girls. They were fine today. Well, okay, at least. It's about me. About something that happened to me when I was five years old."

"When you were five?" Natasha's tired smile said she couldn't believe it. "Don't we have enough to worry about without dredging up something that happened almost nine years ago?"

Rudy felt his voice begin to shake as he said, "I got buried alive, Mom. I got buried and Murph saved my life."

She was listening then, her face tense and pale, as the words that had been rising up all afternoon began to pour out. The words that told about what had happened, and why, and what Art had done and what Murph had done. And how, when it was over, he'd blocked it out of his memory, except for the nightmares and the times when he'd had the attacks of claustrophobia. And how he hadn't really remembered until today when he told Murph about his claustrophobia and Murph decided to tell him the whole story.

Rudy was shaking hard again as he talked and his voice was trembling, but this time right along with the terror there was a kind of easing somewhere down deep, as if something dark and heavy was breaking up and oozing away. Somewhere in the midst of the story, Natasha moved over beside him and put her arms around him, but it wasn't until he'd finished that he realized she was crying.

"Hey, don't do that," Rudy said.

"It's my fault," Natasha sobbed. "It's all my fault."

"No, it isn't. How could it be your fault? You didn't even know about it."

She cried harder then, so hard that for a while she couldn't talk. But when she finally began again it was in short phrases between gasps and sobs. "That's just it —I should have known . . . and I should never have left you with Art—not ever—and I should *never, never* have married him—but I was so young, and it was so hard being a single mother—and he pretended to like you so much until—until it was too late."

"I know. I know all that," Rudy said. "Murph explained it to me years ago. And I think I understood it even before that. I always knew it wasn't your fault."

She cried some more after that, but then she got up and went into the kitchen and washed her face. She was scrubbing it hard with a towel when he came in and she smiled at him in a wobbly, uncertain way.

"Rudy," she said. "I want to talk to Murph, alone. At least for now. Maybe later we'll all talk—the three of us."

"Sure," Rudy said. "I'll be in my room. But call me if you want me. I definitely won't be asleep."

Natasha said okay and hugged him again and went out the back door, and Rudy went to bed. And even though he felt certain he wouldn't even be able to close his eyes, he must have fallen asleep almost immediately.

He woke up the next morning gingerly, aware that something had happened but not remembering exactly what. Then it all came flooding back and to his relief he found that, on the whole, he felt pretty good about it.

What he was feeling was that he'd survived. Survived the cave-in—and learning about it—and talking about it to Natasha, and he'd probably survive talking about it again to Murph and Natasha if that was going to happen sometime soon.

And—though this bit of good news wasn't related to the cave-in thing, it was perhaps even more important—he'd survived the threat of having to choose between becoming a gold miner and losing Barney's friendship for good. Because it certainly seemed possible, judging by the way things were going before Barney left for Montana, that he might be losing interest in Tyler and his hair-ball schemes.

Everything was back to normal at breakfast. Natasha was running late and hurrying, but she hugged him extra hard before she ran out the door and whispered that they'd talk some more that evening. Rudy got the girls off to the sitter's and just a little later the phone rang. It was Barney.

179

"Hey, Barn. You're home," Rudy said. "How was it? Did you have a great time?"

"Yeah, great," Barney said. "The rodeos were great—and the weather, and—everything."

Rudy waited, but he didn't say any more. "Well, tell me about it. Was being in the junior events a blast?"

"Yeah. Sure. A blast. I got to compete in a couple of things in Butte. I got a first in the calf-riding event and a third in roping."

"Wow. Did you get blue ribbons and billions in prize money and like that?"

"Well, ribbons, anyhow. Oh, yeah, and a belt buckle for the first prize. It was—a blast."

"And . . . And . . ."

"And what?"

"What else did you do? Did you go to all the rodeos and watch your mom and dad take a lot of prizes?"

"Oh, sure, you know the world-famous Crookshanks." There was something different about Barney's tone of voice. It sounded almost sarcastic. Except that it wasn't like Barney to be sarcastic about anything. "The famous Crookshanks always pick up some prize money in an event or two—and even when they don't, they always steal the show."

"Barney?" Rudy said. "What's the matter?"

There was a long silence before Barney answered. "Oh, nothing. Just remind me not to go on the circuit with my folks again. Not until I'm eighteen, at least."

"Why's that?"

"Well, it's just that I hardly ever saw them except

180

from the stands. The rest of the time they were with their friends and mostly in places where you have to be eighteen to get in. So I sat around in motel rooms a lot. Alone. Want to know what's on late-night TV in Montana? I can give you a complete rundown."

For once Rudy was speechless. He wanted to say how sorry he was that Barney had such a bad time and he also wanted to say how disgusted it made him that Jeb and Angela had deserted him, again and as usual. But what he actually did was what he always did when he didn't know how to deal with something. He made a joke of it. "Okay," he said. "I'll bite. What's on NBC in Butte, Montana, at eleven thirty? Nothing good, I'll bet."

"Yeah," Barney said. "You got it."

There was another awkward pause, and then Rudy said, "Look, Barney. I do want to talk to you. Could you come in to town?"

"To your place?" Barney sounded uncertain. "I don't know if I have time. I've got something I have to do at twelve."

Rudy looked at the clock. It was ten o'clock and Margot and Moira would be coming home at one. "Well, I could get out to the ranch and back by one, but it wouldn't leave much time for—"

But Barney interrupted. "I didn't mean for you to come here. How about"—his voice lowered—"how about at the mine? It doesn't take as long to get there."

Rudy's throat squeezed up so fast he had to try twice before any sound came out. "The mine?" he said at last.

"Yeah. Pritchard's Hole. I was just talking to Styler a few minutes ago and I'm supposed to meet him there around twelve. He's been working on the entrance—you know, prying off some of the boarding—while I was away. He thinks we could actually get inside today."

"Inside the mine?" Rudy managed to say, fighting to keep his voice at a normal pitch and to control what felt like a series of small explosions that seemed to be happening somewhere inside his skull. It didn't seem possible. Tyler hadn't mentioned the mine even once while Barney was gone. But then he wouldn't, of course, to Rudy. Not if he felt Rudy might rat on him if he didn't have to rat on Barney at the same time—which was probably exactly how he felt.

"Yeah." Barney's voice suddenly sounded odd, higher pitched and with a sharp, excited ring to it. "We're planning to start today. Can you come? You can still be in on it, if you want to be. How about it?"

Rudy took a deep shaky breath, and with a huge effort shut off the explosions and began to think. "Well, I don't know. I can't stay very long because of the baby-sitting. But I do want to . . ." He paused for a minute, his mind racing. "When did you say Tyler's going to be there?"

"He said around twelve."

"Could you get there sooner? Like in about half an hour?"

"Yeah. Sure."

"Okay," Rudy said. "I'll meet you there. At the mine at ten thirty."

Five minutes later Rudy was on his bicycle heading up Lone Pine toward the edge of town where the old Cemetery Road led toward the northeast and Pritchard's Hole. He rode at top speed past all the weatherbeaten old houses that straggled out along Cemetery Road, some of them windowless and empty, and then on into the open countryside. While he raced along his mind was going even faster, going over and over the things he'd been planning to say to Barney. Over what he would need to say in order to make Barney realize that going down into an abandoned mine, not to mention jumping off water towers and swinging across deep canyons, were not things that he really needed, or even wanted to do. It wasn't going to be easy.

It was an extrahot dry day and even before he'd turned off Lone Pine onto Cemetery he was sweating like crazy and there was a fierce catch in his side. He didn't slow down, however, until he'd passed the huge rotting headframe of the old Olympia Mine and reached the really steep part of the road. At last, breathless and gasping, he passed the crest and began to coast down to where another road angled off to the left. More of a trail really, rutted and overgrown by weeds—it was the old wagon track to Pritchard's Hole.

Pushing his bicycle, Rudy made his way through a small grove of trees and out onto a flat open field that ended where the steep rocky foothills began, rising up sharply toward the mountains beyond. The field was scattered with broken bits of debris, the wheel-less remains of an old ore cart, piles of rotting wooden planks, and odds and ends of rusting pipe and rail. And beyond that, set into the cliff face, thick wooden pillars framed the entrance to Pritchard's Hole.

183

Rudy had been there before—once just exploring the area with Barney and Sty, and another time on a kind of neighborhood picnic. He remembered how the heavy weathered planks completely covered the entrance, held in place by huge rusty spikes. But now two of the splintery old planks were missing and in their place was a narrow strip of deep, empty darkness.

Rudy turned his back on the mine and looked around at the scarred and littered field. He walked over to the ore cart and checked it out and then poked around in a pile of broken pipes and tools. There was still no sign of Barney. But as he started toward a thick log that offered a fairly comfortable sitting place, he became aware of the sound of an approaching bicycle. A moment later Barney burst out of the grove and skidded to a stop only a few feet away.

They went through the usual "Hey, Barn" and "Rudy-dudey" more or less in unison and then Rudy gestured toward the other end of the log and added, "Be my guest." Barney propped his bike against the ore cart, took off a bulging backpack and dropped it on the ground, and sat down straddling the log.

His thick blondish hair was hanging down into his eyes as usual, and his slow, crooked grin was just getting underway when Rudy said, "Look, Barney. I've got to talk to you about something very important and there isn't much time. It's about . . . it's about this gold-mining deal."

Barney's smile faded. "Yeah, what about it?"

"Well, the thing is, I can't do it."

He hadn't meant to start that way. He'd intended

to begin by talking about why some people feel com-
pelled to do dangerous things, not because they really
want to but in order to prove something or just to get
someone's attention. But sitting there, staring Barney
in the face, he suddenly knew that what he'd planned
to say wouldn't go over very well. What he'd been ig-
noring was how much Barney hated any kind of pok-
ing around in his personal feelings. And the only other
approach that Rudy could come up with in a hurry
was to tell why he, himself, couldn't possibly be involved. Admitting to Barney that he had something as
weird as claustrophobia wasn't easy, but on the other
hand if Barn was really feeling sorry for him he might
not be so quick to get mad at him for what he was
going to say next.

"You can't?" Barney looked puzzled.

"That's right. Well, the thing is, I got caught in a
cave-in once and it almost killed me, and now I really
lose it if I go in any kind of dark, closed-in place."
Even saying just that much made Rudy's heartbeat
pick up the pace a little.

"Cave-in?" Barney looked puzzled. "You never
told me about any cave-in before."

"Yeah, I know. I'd forgotten about it. It's called
repression, which means your mind just kind of wipes
out something that's too painful to remember. And besides, I was unconscious right afterward and when I
came to I just didn't remember. Except in dreams. I've
kind of remembered it in dreams ever since."

He went on then, telling the whole story of the
cave-in and the part Murph had played and how
Murph had been the one to finally tell him about it.

It still wasn't easy talking about it. As soon as he began his shoulders started to quiver, and he could feel a gathering tightness in his head and chest. But he went on talking and finally he couldn't help being pleased at how well he was doing. Although his voice got wobbly and his heart was pounding a bit, he didn't come nearly as unglued as he had before.

The whole time he was talking Barney listened very carefully, now and then shaking his head and saying, "wow," and "yeah," and "unreal."

Rudy wound up by saying, "So anyway, that's why I can't help out with the gold mining. I mean, I couldn't do it if I knew for absolute certain that old Rooney knew what he was talking about and we were going to find a million dollars' worth of gold nuggets. Which, by the way, I don't believe for a minute."

Barney nodded slowly. Then he grinned and said, "Hey, it's okay. I mean, this gold-mining thing isn't going to take the whole summer. There's a lot of other stuff we can do." He got up, grabbed his backpack, and started taking things out of it, a small sharp pointed pick and a coil of rope and then a miner's helmet with a flashlight taped on top of it. He put the helmet down on the ground and started rearranging the other stuff in the pack.

"Wait a minute," Rudy said. "That's not all I wanted to talk about."

"Yeah?" Barney sat back down on the log with the rope in his hands, and as Rudy went on talking he started untying the knot that held it in a coil. "Shoot," he said.

Rudy took a slow breath and began. "It's about

why *you* want to do this gold-mining stuff. I mean, you
know as well as I do that the chances of your finding
any gold down there are pretty much in the fat-chance
range. And you also know that breaking into abandoned mines is against the law, not to mention being
about as safe as skateboarding on the freeway. I mean,
I'm talking world-class, terminally dangerous, Barn."

Barney had been frowning, but now suddenly he
started to smile. Not his normal easygoing grin, but a
tense, tight-lipped grimace, and Rudy knew immediately that he'd taken the wrong tack. He should have
known that telling Barney that something was too dangerous was like waving a red flag in front of a bull.
There was something in Barney that *wanted* danger the
way a junkie wants a fix.

"Wait a minute," Rudy said. "There's something
else I want to say. I just want to ask you *why* you want
to do it? I know why Styler wants to do it. Partly to get
rid of me because he could see I wasn't going to do it.
But also because he really and truly thinks he's going
to get rich, and he is completely and totally hung up
on money. But it's not that way with you. I know that.
I know you better than that."

"So." Barney's eyes had narrowed, but the tense
excited look still was there. "What else do you think
you know about me?"

Rudy took a deep breath. "Well, I think you've
been trying to prove something."

"Prove something?"

"Yeah. Not just with this mine thing either. With
other things like when we made that swing over the
gulch, and dove off the water tower, and lots of stuff

like that. I think you were trying to prove something then too. To yourself and perhaps even more to—to your parents."

"Like what?" Barney's voice was low and flat.

"Like, that you're just as brave and daring and glamorous as they are."

"So, you think I'm jealous of my parents, is that it?"

"No. Not jealous. It's more like . . . well, maybe you think . . . I mean sort of subconsciously . . . that if you do something really dangerous and prove how brave you are, they'll start . . . well, paying more attention to you." Rudy found himself talking faster and faster as Barney's face got harder and tighter. "That's what Natasha says that Belle thought about you. She thought you were just trying to get your parents to care about you. And she said the reason you used to go to sleep in the daytime all the time was because you were so worried about your folks being gone so much that you couldn't sleep at night and—"

Barney stood up suddenly and threw the coiled rope. He threw it more or less down at the ground, but also at Rudy's legs. Rudy had never seen him look so angry.

"So that's what you and your mom have been saying about me, huh? And who else have you been talking to about me? Half of Pyramid Hill? And what else have you been telling them? I suppose you've been telling them all about the mine and the gold and what Ty and I are planning to do."

Rudy stood up, too, very slowly. In a quiet voice

he said, "You know I wouldn't do that, Barney. You know that. I haven't told anyone—"

"Look," Barney broke in. "I've got stuff to do. I'm going to go into that mine in a few minutes and I have to get ready. So you better get out of here. Go on, get out. Now."

Rudy got on his bike and left. All the way home he kept thinking the same thing over and over. *You blew it, Drummond. You really blew it this time.*

Chapter 17

I T WAS ONLY about three hours after Rudy rode off and left Barney alone at Pritchard's Hole, that someone banged on the back door of the Drummond house while another doll game was in progress at the kitchen table.

The game had been going on for quite a while without anything interesting happening and Rudy had more or less tuned out, using only half his mind to make the Rudy troll doll answer questions with noes and yesses. The other half was busy worrying about Barney. He'd just finished telling himself for the hundredth time that Barney would get over being mad at him and there was no use thinking about what might happen in the mine because there was nothing he could do about it, when someone ran up the back steps and pounded on the door so hard it rattled the hinges.

Rudy quickly dropped the troll doll and got up from the table—not being particularly anxious to be seen playing dolls. But when Margot rushed to the door and threw it open he forgot to worry about whether he'd been seen. It was Tyler Lewis.

Ty's face was bright red and dripping with sweat and he was gasping for breath. He looked like he'd been running—or riding his bike—at top speed in the hot sun. But there was more to it than that. Ty was definitely excited about something—or angry—or *frightened.* "Barney?" Rudy asked. "Is something wrong with Barney?"

Ty looked around Rudy at Moira and Margot, and then stepped backward, motioning for Rudy to follow. It wasn't until Rudy closed the door behind him that Tyler said, "No, Barney's all right. He—he just wants to talk to you. He sent me to get you. He said to tell you it's very important."

"Where is he?" Rudy asked.

"At the mine," Ty said. "He's out by the mine."

Rudy was puzzled—and suspicious. "If Barney wants to talk to me why doesn't he come tell me so himself?"

Tyler shrugged impatiently. "I don't know. He's doing something real important and—"

But then something occurred to Rudy. "Did he tell you about . . . well, about what happened this morning?"

Ty's eyes narrowed. "Maybe," he said. "What happened to who?"

"To Barney and me. About the . . . well, the fight we had."

"Oh, that." Ty nodded. "Yeah, he told me. That's probably what he wants to see you about. Something about the fight. Maybe he wants to say he's sorry."

See, Rudy told himself. *I told you he wouldn't stay mad very long.* To Ty he said, "Okay. I'll come. If I can get someone to take care of my sisters."

Inside the kitchen he went to the phone and called Eleanora.

"Hi, Eleanora," he said, talking loudly to be heard over the uproar of playing kids. "This is Rudy. Hey, look. Something real important has come up and I'm going to have to go take care of it. Could I send the girls back for the afternoon?"

"Well, sure," Eleanora's loud good-natured voice boomed out over the cheerful shrieking and yelling. "If it's really important. Just send them along. Tell them I'll be expecting them in fifteen minutes. Okay?"

So a few minutes later Moira and Margot were on their way back to the baby-sitter's and Rudy and Tyler were on their bikes heading back to Pritchard's Hole. They didn't talk much on the way there. It was very hot and they were riding fast, and besides, Rudy's mind was busy with other things, like wondering why Barney would send Ty for him, and what he was going to say about the fight—and if he really did want to apologize for telling Rudy to get out. Or if there was a possibility, maybe, that Barney wanted him there to back him up, to be on his side when he told Ty that he'd changed his mind about doing something so seriously illegal as breaking into an abandoned mine.

Rudy hoped that was it. He was rehearsing what he might tell Tyler about what a breaking and entering charge could do to someone who was just one bust away from juvenile hall, when they came out of the oak grove into the open field. There was no sign of Barney.

Rudy got off his bike and looked around. "Where's Barney?" he said. Then he looked at Ty, and suddenly he knew. "Where's Barney?" he shouted.

"I don't know," Ty wouldn't meet Rudy's eyes. "I think—I think maybe he's somewhere in the mine."

"In the mine? You mean you went off and left him alone in the mine?"

"No. That is, I didn't go in with him. I was supposed to meet him here and I was a little later than I said I'd be. Not a lot, just half an hour or so, but when I got out here he was already gone."

Rudy had to swallow hard before he was able to say, "You sure he didn't just go on home?"

Ty shook his head. "I thought of that, but look. There's his bike over by the cart."

"And all his mining stuff? Where's his helmet and pick and everything?"

Ty nodded. "Gone," he said.

"And you didn't go in after him?"

"Yeah, I did. I went in pretty far. Well, a little way. But I couldn't find him and there are these tunnels branching off in other directions and I didn't know which way he'd gone. So I decided to come and get you." Tyler looked embarrassed. "You know," he said, "it's better to have two people. I mean, if he's hurt or something it would probably take two of us to get him out."

Anger, hot and thick, rose up in Rudy's throat, almost choking him. "If he's hurt or something," he said in a tight voice, "we should have called the police and an ambulance."

"No!" Tyler said quickly. "We can't do that. If we'd done that I'd be terminally busted. And so would Barney. Don't forget that. So would Barney! And besides, he's probably not hurt. He's probably having a ball down there digging out gold nuggets. He's got a copy of the map old Rooney made for me, so he's probably digging away already." Tyler was babbling, the words tumbling out all over each other. "Yeah, that's it. He's probably so busy finding gold that he didn't even hear me when I shouted and—"

"You shouted and he didn't answer?"

"Well, yeah, but like I say—"

"Wait a minute," Rudy said. "Do you have a copy of the map?"

Ty's hand went toward his pocket. "Yeah. I have one."

"Then why didn't you just follow it to where the gold is supposed to be? You'd probably have found him if you did that."

"I tried to. But it was real complicated. The turns and things didn't seem to match the ones on the map. I couldn't figure it out."

"Then what makes you think Barney was able to follow it? If the map is no good then why do you think he was able to go right to the gold? Tell me that. Tell me that," Rudy said and almost added, *"you cement-headed lamebrain."*

He was angry, angrier than he'd ever remembered being. Angry at Ty for starting the whole stupid gold-mine thing in the first place, and absolutely furious at him for lying about why he wanted Rudy to come out to the mine, so Rudy would come alone instead of calling the police.

Rudy grabbed the flashlight Ty was getting out of his backpack and crawled through the opening left by the missing planks, without even stopping to wonder if he was going to be able to do it. He was already standing inside the mine before he felt it beginning. Before the terror started, turning his heartbeat into crazy explosions and tightening his aching throat around an awful need to scream. He was starting to turn back frantically toward the light and air, when Tyler lurched against him, nearly knocking him down.

"Look out," Tyler shouted. "Bats. Bats."

When Rudy regained his balance Tyler was crouching beside him, his arms waving wildly around his head. He was wearing a helmet with a flashlight taped on top of it and he had a small pickax in one hand. "Bats," he was still shouting. "Look out. Bats!"

A jabbing pain shot up Rudy's arm as the waving pickax hit him sharply on the elbow. It was about to get him again when he grabbed it and wrenched it out of Tyler's hand. "Stop it!" he yelled. "What's the matter?"

"Bats," Tyler was whispering now, pointing up over their heads. And then Rudy saw them, too, two small dark shapes that flitted around them and then darted out through the entrance and disappeared.

Rudy turned the flashlight on the ceiling of the mine tunnel. Jagged gray rocks gleamed darkly between the old planks of a rotten wooden frame. Near the entrance thick curtains of spiderweb swayed slightly, but nothing else moved. No flitting wings or glittering eyes.

"They're gone," Rudy said. "I think the bats are gone." He looked down to where Tyler still crouched on the floor. His eyes, shining out from under the edge of the helmet, were still wide and jittery.

"Have you got a thing about bats too?" Rudy asked.

Tyler stood up. He straightened his helmet and grabbed his pick out of Rudy's hand. "What do you mean, a thing?" he said. "I just don't like them is all. They fly into your hair or down your neck if they get a chance. I just don't like them."

Rudy stared at him, wondering if bats were the reason he'd given up on finding Barney by himself, if seeing some bats was why he'd only gone "a little way" before he decided to go for help. "Which way did you go before?" Rudy asked.

Tyler pulled the map out of his pocket. Spreading it out with shaky hands, he pointed out how you were supposed to go down the main tunnel past two very short cross tunnels that took off to the left, and then turn down another long tunnel to the right. "But something's not right," he said. "There aren't any short tunnels. The first turn off goes to the right and it looks like it goes on forever."

Rudy studied the map, turning it from side to side. It looked to him like a blurry, mixed-up mess. He couldn't believe that this useless scribble made Tyler and Barney think the old miner knew what he was talking about. "Come on," he said. "Forget about the map. Let's just start walking. And calling."

Rudy took a deep breath. The air was cool and dank and smelled of earth and decay. He turned the flashlight down the tunnel ahead of them, illuminating ancient scaffolding and rough rocky walls that seemed to lean inward, soaking up the feeble light. He had only gone a few steps when the throat-tightening, chest-squeezing terror started up again, stopping him in his tracks. Gasping for air, Rudy closed his eyes tightly and screamed.

"Barney!" he shouted with every ounce of power in his throat and lungs. The force of the yell stretched his lungs, pained his throat—and somehow seemed to dull the inward ache of terror. He plunged ahead down the tunnel.

A few yards down the main passageway a smaller one went off to the right. Rudy turned up it, but after he'd gone a few yards he stopped and came back. Grabbing the pick out of Ty's hands he hacked a rough arrow into the stone to mark their path. Then he again started up the smaller tunnel.

Here they had to move very slowly. The footing was rough and uneven, and the ceiling was so low they often had to walk in a crouching position. This branch of the mine seemed to be sloping upward and as they went the air became drier and a little warmer. Every few feet they stopped to call.

Whenever the terror began to build up, Rudy called—screamed—for Barney, and the black panic backed away. He could still feel it, though, hiding like a dark cloud around the edges of his mind, waiting to force its way out. But the shouting helped to hold it at bay and, in a strange way, so did Tyler. Lurching against Rudy, grabbing his arm from time to time and continually babbling about bats, Tyler's presence was as constant as the lurking terror's, and just about as much of a nuisance.

They had been walking for some time when they came to a place where part of the roof had given way and collapsed onto the tunnel floor. A scattering of rocks and earth covered the floor for several feet. Tyler clutched Rudy's arm.

"Barney?" he said in a horrified tone of voice, pointing to the largest pile of debris. For a moment Rudy's heart thudded up into his throat, but then he shook his head. The rockfall wasn't big enough to hide an entire body. If Barney had been under it at least his feet and legs would be visible.

"No," he said. "I don't think so." He studied the area around the rockfall a moment longer before he added, "I don't even think he came this way. Look at the dust."

"Hey," Tyler said, "You're right. Look behind us."

The air was dry here and a thick, smooth layer of dust had settled over the rockfall and the tunnel floor. Behind them their two sets of footprints were clearly visible, but up ahead the dust was smooth and undisturbed. No one had come this way in many years. They turned around quickly and made their way back to the main tunnel.

Unlike the side passageway, the central one sloped downward. The air was colder and water oozed along the walls and dripped from the ceiling. As they moved forward they splashed through shallow pools of muddy water, and ducked under great overhanging clumps of shiny wet rock. Now and then they stopped to shout and to chip an arrow into the wall to mark their way. But their calls weren't answered. They only echoed again and again, fading away gradually to the terrible unearthly silence.

As they moved forward the surface beneath their feet began to slant downward more rapidly, and the slope oozed with slimy water. They had to walk carefully, groping for footholds that would keep them from sliding. They hadn't called for several minutes when Tyler suddenly said, "Listen."

Rudy stopped quickly. Ty crashed into him and they both slipped and slid, grabbing each other before they finally regained their balance. For a moment there was nothing but the awful silence, but then they heard it. A faint faraway voice calling "Help."

"Barney," Rudy called, but relief and joy made his voice wobble and he had to swallow hard and try again. "Barney. We're coming. Where are you?" he yelled and plunged forward on the slippery surface.

They hurried on, slipping and sliding, and as they went Barney's answering calls grew louder. "Rudy," he called, and "Tyler. Here I am. I can't get out." And then, "Be careful. Watch where you step. Go slow."

Underfoot the slope was even steeper and the

slimy mud covered everything. Barney's voice was very near when suddenly the slant changed direction. There was a sharp sideways turn and then, at what seemed to be the entrance to another side tunnel, a sharp drop into darkness.

Bracing himself against the wall, Rudy was creeping forward when his foot hit something that clattered ahead of him. It was a pickax, Barney's probably. Rudy dropped to his knees and crawled forward, bracing himself against the tunnel wall. When he reached the brink he leaned forward and shone the flashlight down into a deep pit—and directly onto Barney's upturned face.

"Hey, Barn," Rudy tried to say, choked, and tried again. "Hey, Barn. Are you all right?"

Barney didn't answer immediately. His face twitched and he gasped and choked, and when he finally did speak his voice was shaky. "Yeah," he said. "I'm all right—now. Just get me out of here."

The pit Barney had fallen into wasn't deep. Lying on his stomach and reaching down, Rudy could almost touch Barney's outstretched fingers. But the wall was steep and slippery with oozing water. Barney jumped several times, reaching up desperately toward Rudy's hands, and then splashing back down into the deep puddle on the pit floor.

"The rope," he gasped finally, and pawing around in the dark water around his feet he located his rope, and threw one end up to Rudy. Then, with Rudy and Ty holding one end, Barney held the rope with both hands while his feet scrabbled and slipped against the wall. When that didn't work he tied the rope around his waist so that his hands were free. But there were no useful handholds, and even with both Rudy and Ty pulling he made no progress. Instead Rudy and Ty were nearly dragged down into the pit themselves. Finally Rudy thought of the pickaxes.

"Hey, wait," he said. "I'm going to dig us some footholds so we can brace ourselves. And maybe you can chip some out too. Down there on the wall. Some holes you can get your toes and fingers into."

"But I don't have my pickax," Barney said. "I had it in my hand when I slipped and fell, and I dropped it. It's somewhere up there."

So they found Barney's pickax and threw it down to him, and with Rudy and Ty taking turns with the other they began to dig. But the rock was hard and progress was slow. It seemed like hours before the holes were deep enough to be useful and they were ready to try again. This time Rudy and Ty sat down facing the pit, dug their heels into the freshly dug excavations, and pulled with all their strength. And down below Barney, with the rope tied around his waist, slipped and scrambled on the wall—slipped down and tried again—and again—and then his hands appeared on the ledge, and then his arms and finally his dented helmet with its weakly shining flashlight above his wet, dirt-smeared face. He slithered toward them on his stomach, dragged himself to his knees— and lurched forward on top of Rudy and Ty. After that they all three went a little bit crazy.

Grabbing each other, they hugged and pounded, laughing and screaming hysterically. They were still clutched together like some kind of berserk six-legged animal as they slipped and staggered and shouted all the way back up the tunnel.

"Look! A light!" Rudy yelled when they rounded a corner and got their first glimpse of the narrow swath of light at the entrance. He fell to his knees and crawled forward, doing an imitation of a thirst-crazed traveler approaching an oasis in the desert. And Barney and Tyler imitated him, staggering toward the opening yelling, "A light. A light." It wasn't until they had all three crawled out into the hot sunlight that something changed, and the laughter disappeared.

As soon as he was out of the mine Barney sank down in front of the boarding. He took off his helmet and put it at his feet and then he leaned forward with his dirt-smeared face against his knees. He was wet and muddy and shivering so hard his shoulders jerked back and forth. His breath came in ragged gasps. Rudy sat down on one side of him and Tyler on the other. It was quite a while before Barney raised his head.

"I kept waiting for my flashlight to go out," he said. "I thought I was going to die there. In the dark. I was going to lie down in that dirty water—in the dark —and die."

Rudy didn't say anything and neither did Tyler. There didn't seem to be anything to say. It wasn't until quite a while later that Barney spoke again. This time it was just to Rudy. "How'd you do it?" he asked.

"How did I do what?"

"Go down there. You know. I thought you said you couldn't do it."

"Yeah. That's what I thought. I guess I was wrong."

Barney grinned back weakly. "Yeah. I guess you were." He looked at Rudy—a long steady look before he ducked his head and said, "I guess I've been wrong about some stuff too. A lot of stuff."

"Wrong about what?" Ty asked.

But Barney only stood up and picked up his helmet. He took hold of the flashlight and ripped it loose and then he turned around and threw the helmet as far as he could back into the mine. Then he did the same with Tyler's. And Tyler didn't try to stop him.

"I'm coming back tomorrow to nail those boards back up," he said. "But right now I'm going home." Then he got on his bicycle and rode off.

Chapter 18

WHEN RUDY GOT HOME from Pritchard's Hole, covered with dried mud and absolutely exhausted, he barely had time to get cleaned up before Moira and Margot came back from the baby-sitter, and Natasha got home from work. He made an effort to act normal, but it wasn't easy. A strange reaction seemed to have set in and he was feeling a little weird. For one thing it was almost impossible for him to keep his mind on what was going on around him, because scenes from the gold mine kept rerunning on what seemed to be a giant screen located somewhere inside his head.

He managed to say he was okay when Natasha asked him what was the matter, and when Margot mentioned being sent back to Eleanora's he explained by saying he had had to help Barney with something.

Of course, Moira wanted to know what he and Barney had been doing, but he just said it had been a lot of work and he was tired and he'd tell them about it later if they really wanted to know. So Moira said okay and forgot about it. However, it seemed to him that Natasha kept on watching him whenever she thought he wasn't looking.

As soon as Natasha had finished putting the girls to bed, she came back into the kitchen and said, "I'm going to call Murph now. I think the three of us ought to talk—you know, about what happened."

"About what happened?" Rudy asked, startled, because for a split second he found himself wondering how Natasha knew about Pritchard's Hole, and if he'd said something that gave it away. He hoped he hadn't. Not until he'd told Barney he was going to, anyway, and got his okay.

But of course that wasn't it. What Natasha wanted to talk about wasn't what happened that day at Pritchard's Hole. What she was planning to discuss was something that happened nine years ago—in a tunnel dug into the tailings at the Jefferson Mine. "Oh, that," Rudy said, grinning. "I'd almost forgotten about all that."

But Natasha was already on the phone. "Murph," she said, "can you come over now? Yes, anytime. Okay. And for cheesecake and coffee too."

A few minutes later Murph knocked, stuck his head in the back door, and said, "What's this I hear about cheesecake?"

Natasha had hardly poured the coffee before she began about the cave-in. "It's been on my mind all day," she said. "I almost drove Frank crazy—not hearing anything he said to me until he'd repeated it half a dozen times."

"Serves the old slave driver right," Murph said.

Natasha gave Murph a quick smile, then said, "No, seriously, Murph, I just can't stop thinking about what happened and what might have happened and how much I was to blame. And how much I am to blame for not even realizing that Rudy had a problem all these years. Even that time when I came home and he'd been locked in the closet I just put it down to a temper tantrum. But I should have known better. Rudy never has out-of-control temper tantrums. Margot, yes, but not Rudy."

"Now, wait a minute, Natasha," Murph said. "You're being way too hard on yourself. Millions of mothers who've had a much easier time of it than you do a poorer job with their kids. It's always seemed to me that you've done real well with Rudy, considering. Right, Rudy?"

"What?" Rudy said, struggling to deal with what Murph was saying and at the same time a close-up of Barney's frantic face staring up out of the darkness. "What? Oh, yeah. Absolutely. Best mother in Pyramid Hill. Absolutely."

"And as far as the claustrophobia goes, it seems to me that it doesn't have to be a big handicap in Rudy's life. It shouldn't be too hard for him to simply avoid situations that might trigger a panic episode. And I wouldn't be surprised if the whole problem gradually lessens now that it's all out in the open and can be talked about. Just talking it out seems to help some

206

people a great deal. But, of course, at some point he might want to see a psychologist about it too—"

"A psychologist," Rudy interrupted. "We can't afford a psychologist. And besides, I don't think I need one. I think the important thing for me is getting things out in the open and talking about them, just like you said. Like, I've been talking about the cave-in thing a lot since you told me about it. To both of you, and to Barney too. I told Barney about it today, and I think I might be getting over it already. The whole claustrophobia problem, I mean."

"Do you?" Natasha looked pleased. "Why? Did something happen today that made you think you were getting over it?"

But he couldn't get into that one. "Sure," he said. "Today some things happened, but that's not the important part. What's important is I've been doing a lot more talking to people lately and I've been finding out all kinds of stuff that might help. And not only me. Things that might help other people too."

"That might help what other people?" Natasha was looking puzzled.

"Well, like Barney for instance, and Ty. And the girls too. I've been talking a lot more to Moira and Margot lately and I've found out some interesting facts about—well, about why they fight so much, for one thing."

"Is that right?" Murph said. "I'd be interested to hear about that one."

"And so would I," Natasha said. "God knows, so would I."

"Sure," Rudy said. "I might have some really important information on the subject. What I think is we ought to have some more discussions like this—I mean, every once in a while." He pushed back his chair and stood up. "But right at this particular moment I am really beat. I mean terminally wasted. So if nobody minds I'm going to go to bed. Why don't you guys go right on talking? I mean about how certain people have to knock off this 'it's all my fault' bit. What I think is you really ought to talk some more about that, Murph." And Rudy staggered down the hall and fell into bed.

The next morning he had just gotten Moira and Margot off to the sitter's when someone knocked on the front door. This time it was Barney himself. An almost completely back to normal Barney in his old beat-up L.A. Gear sneakers and jeans and his usual cool and easy grin, with nothing showing that would give away what had happened to him just the day before, except for some raw-looking places on the ends of his fingers and a big scab on one elbow.

"Hey, Rudy," he said. "What's up?"

"Nothing much," Rudy said. "I just got the two little dweebs off to Eleanora's. What's up with you?"

Barney shrugged and lowered himself onto the veranda railing. "Nothing much. I just came over because —well, because I want to say something."

"You do?" Rudy did a "big surprise" bit. "To say something? Barney Crookshank actually wants to say something. Well, okay, shoot. Feel free. Be my guest."

Barney frowned. "Quit kidding around for a minute, will you? What I want to say is . . . well, it's a lot more than just thanks. I mean, how do you thank somebody who does the hardest thing in the world for you? I mean, the thing you said you couldn't do for a billion dollars."

"A million," Rudy said. "I said I couldn't do it for a million." He nodded thoughtfully. "For a billion, maybe. Anyway, like you said, I was wrong. Maybe it wasn't as hard as I thought it was going to be."

Barney took off one of his L.A. Gear sneakers, shook it, and took out a big pebble. Then, rolling the pebble between his skinned-up fingers, he said, "How'd you happen to be out there anyway? I mean, after I told you to get out?"

So Rudy told him about how Ty had come for him. And how Ty tricked him into coming with him instead of calling the police, and then he went on talking a little more, and without really meaning to he got into the thing about Ty and the bats.

"Ty went into the mine looking for me and then he left and went off to get you because he was afraid of the bats?" Barney said. "He didn't say anything about any of that to me—when I called him, I mean."

"You called Ty this morning?" Rudy asked.

"Yeah. I told him to come here." Barney looked at his watch. "He ought to be here by now."

Rudy didn't ask why. He wanted to, but he didn't. And it was only a few minutes later that they heard Ty's bicycle and then there he was, coming up the steps in a pair of flashy knee-length shorts and a T-shirt that had TAKE A CHILL PILL written across the front.

"Yo, dudes," he said, kicking back on Natasha's lounge chair with his arms behind his head. "What's going down?" He was doing his usual cocky grin, but it did seem to wobble a little as he looked up at Barney and said, "You wanted to see me about something, Barn?"

"Yeah." Barney was still rolling the pebble around in his raw-looking fingers. "I wanted to talk to both of you. About the mine. I just wanted to say the whole thing is off, at least as far as I'm concerned."

"Sure, Barn," Ty said. "You didn't have to drag me over here to tell me that. I mean, I got the picture yesterday. Loud and clear. It's okay with me. Hell, there's a lot of other things we can get into now that you're back in town." He glanced at Rudy. "I mean, things were pretty slow around here last week. I tried to get something started with old 'Chickie-baby' here, but a kiddie movie or two was about as good as it got."

Barney went on looking down at the pebble, rolling it in his fingers. Then he got up slowly and went over to where Ty was stretched out on the lounge chair. He stood there staring down at Ty for so long that Rudy started feeling antsy, and from the look on Ty's face, he did too. Then Barney reached down, took hold of Ty's chin, pulled it down, held the pebble that came out of his shoe over Ty's mouth—and dropped it in. He put his fist under Ty's chin and pushed until Ty's mouth shut and his head went back—way back.

"Shut your mouth, Styler," he said in a hard, tight voice. "Shut your mouth for keeps on that Chickie stuff or . . . or maybe I'll think up a new name for you. Like 'Bats,' maybe. That's it. Yeah. I just might start calling you 'Bats.'"

"Hey, okay," Ty said as soon as Barney took his

fist away. He sat up and took the pebble out of his mouth and stared at it for a minute. Then he looked sideways at Rudy. "Sorry about that, Rudy," he said. "Anyway, all I meant to say was we can have a lot more fun now that old Barn is back. Right?" He glanced at Rudy again and added, "The three of us can have a lot more fun."

"Sure we can," Rudy said, and the funny part was he kind of meant it. He meant it because he suddenly realized that if old Styler were to disappear forever he'd miss him, at least a little. He wasn't too sure just why, but maybe it was simply that surviving Tyler Lewis had become a kind of challenge. Maybe he needed Ty—like a mountain climber needs the Matterhorn, or a snake charmer needs a six-foot cobra.

Right after that Tyler said he was going to Sacramento with his parents and he needed to get right home. He got on his twenty-one-speed bicycle and started off up Lone Pine shifting gears like crazy. Rudy and Barney watched him go and when he'd disappeared over the rise Rudy brought up something he hadn't gotten up the nerve to ask about before.

"I was wondering, Barn," he started out. "Well, the thing is that I've been talking to Murph a lot lately, and Natasha too. Like I told you, Murph saved me when I was in the cave-in, and I've been talking to him about that. And I was just wondering if it would be all right if I told him about Pritchard's Hole—I mean now that it's all over?"

Barney had gone back to sit on the railing. "Sure," he said. "You can tell them. I told Granddad last night."

"You did?" Rudy was amazed. "What did he say?"

Barney grinned. "Well, you know Granddad. He didn't say much. Just that he was glad I told him, and that he hoped it had learned me a lesson. And I said I thought it had."

"And your mom and dad? Did you tell them too?"

"Nope. They weren't home, as usual."

Rudy nodded and Barney looked at him—long and level—and then he nodded too. And Rudy knew the nod meant something important and he thought he knew what. They sat quietly for a moment and then Barney unwound his long legs and got up. "I better get going," he said. "I have to run some errands in town for Granddad."

He was partway down the steps when Rudy called to him. When he turned back Rudy said, "I was just wondering if you'd like to be here when I talk to Murph and Natasha? I mean, about Pritchard's Hole—and everything."

Barney's smile disappeared and he began to shake his head.

"Come on, Barn. You'd better say yes. I'll tell a bunch of lies about you if you don't."

But Barney didn't smile. He looked at Rudy and then down at his feet and then he ran his hand through his hair and down the back of his neck. Then he raised his chin up high, just the way he'd done in kindergarten when all the kids were expecting him to cry. "Okay. Okay, I'll be here. You call and tell me when and I'll come."

212

When Barney left, Rudy went back to lying in the hammock for a while. Thinking. He thought first about Barney and how it hard it would be for him to talk to Murph and Natasha, or to anybody, about anything personal. But he'd said yes because—well, probably because Rudy had asked him to.

Just then Ophelia came back from escorting the girls to the sitter's, and that got him started thinking about Margot and Moira and what Moira had told him about her problem with teasing people. He was still thinking about Moira when a horn tooted and there was Heather driving by in her new Toyota. He waved and she waved back and drove on up Lone Pine—and then he thought about Heather, and Barney's crush on her, and the riding lessons. And then Ty's riding lesson that wound up in the hedge—and a bunch of other stuff about Ty.

He was still thinking about Ty's problems—with bats, being homeless, and Shetland Ponies from Hell, when he heard the slam of a screen door and there was Murph shuffling across his veranda in his bedroom slippers, carrying a watering can.

Murph came down the south side of his house watering his geraniums and when he got across from the hammock he nodded and said good morning.

"Hi, Murph," Rudy said.

"Noticed you there in the hammock," Murph said.

"I'll bet you did. And I'll bet you thought I was just goofing off. Didn't you?"

"But you weren't, I'm sure."

"No, I wasn't. Not at all. What I was doing, actu-

213

ally, was studying humanity. Yeah, that's it. I was studying humanity. It's my new research project."

"I see." Murph was grinning. "Well, let me know if I can be of any assistance."

"Okay," Rudy said. "I sure will."

ZILPHA KEATLEY SNYDER has written many distinguished books for children, including *The Egypt Game, The Headless Cupid,* and *The Witches of Worm,* all Newbery Honor Books and American Library Association Notable Books for Children. Her most recent books for Delacorte Press are *Song of the Gargoyle* and *Libby on Wednesday.*

Zilpha Keatley Snyder lives in Marin County, California.